A CANDLELIGHT ROMANCE

CANDLELIGHT ROMANCES

PORTRAIT OF LOVE

Jean Hager

A CANDLELIGHT ROMANCE

For Mother . . .
And in loving memory of Granddad
and my other Cherokee ancestors

Published by
Dell Publishing Co., Inc.
1 Dag Hammarskjold Plaza
New York, New York 10017

Dell ® TM 681510, Dell Publishing Co., Inc.

ISBN: 0-440-17013-3

Printed in the United States of America
First printing—February 1981

1

Jordan did not like lawyers' offices. He had started to dislike them during his first year of law school, and by the time of his graduation they had begun to have a decidedly claustrophobic effect on him.

He shifted his long frame in the uncomfortable leather chair and longed for the trees and rocky hills of his country place sixty miles away in the remote reaches of Cherokee County. He was aware of the middle-aged secretary's furtive glances in his direction as she pounded her typewriter keys. She knew who he was, of course, and evidently was impressed by the presence in her office of the famous Cherokee painter, Jordan Ridge. Further, if Jordan had but known it, she thought his tall, elegantly suited figure and darkly brooding features quite appropriate to his reputation. She would never have suspected that he felt more at home rambling over his rustic acres in patched jeans and faded shirts.

Jordan himself had long ago given up wishing he could be other than as he was, even though his defection from a similarly paneled law office had disappointed and bewildered his now-dead parents. In retrospect, it was their ambition for him that had propelled him into law school in the first place.

To be perfectly honest, Jordan had once dreamed of helping Indian people with his legal training, but, as low man in the firm where he was employed, he felt unable to be a real force in lifting up a downtrodden people. To relieve some of the frustration, he had returned to the pastime of his younger years, painting, not as a hobbyist this time, but as a serious student. He had tried landscapes while studying the English painters, and Christian themes while immersing himself in the work of the Italian masters.

Then he had met Asudi Vann, an old Cherokee story-teller, cherisher and purveyor of oral tribal history and myth—one of the last of a vanishing breed. . . .

Jordan got to his feet, stretched his cramped body, and went to stand in front of the wall of books, pretending to study the titles. Had it really been more than eight years since that crisp October evening when he had camped out on the banks of Coyote Creek? Having reached a crossroad in his life, he had backpacked into his native Oklahoma hills to ponder which direction he should take. Although a noble and useful profession, the practice of law was not for him. Painting was the thing that drew him, but he had to make a living and, up to that time, his imitations of the styles of the masters had not brought in much money.

It was growing dark that October evening and he had built a campfire to roast the rabbit he'd found in his make-shift trap. An elderly Cherokee man had appeared in the light of the campfire, his aged brown face leathered by wind and rain, his dark eyes deep and melancholy.

Jordan had urged him to partake of his rabbit and cof-fee, and the old man had accepted with gracious reticence. He said that he was Asudi Vann and that he lived on his farm "over yonder"—the direction indicated by the pointing of gnarled old fingers. Upon learning Jordan's identity, he said he had known Jordan's parents, who had died the year before.

Before the shared meal was finished, Jordan found him-self pouring out to Asudi his depression and frustration over his continued failure as an artist, a failure that was not merely financial, for even then Jordan sensed that the im-ages that flowed from his brush had no life in them, but were merely shadows of other people's reality.

Asudi had sat as unmoving as a statue, listening to Jor-dan's unhappy tale for a long time. When Jordan had talked himself out, the old man started to speak: "Everything is just as the Great Spirit planned. He made everything the way it is, even you, Jordan Ridge. I believe you know already what your heart is telling you. It is the Great Spirit's voice—here." He touched a brown hand to his chest. "You must listen."

Jordan laughed cynically. "Then he is telling me to paint, but he has not told me how I am to make a living."

Solemnly, Asudi nodded. "It may be that you do not paint the proper things. You are Cherokee by blood, although I think not by upbringing. Still the blood of your ancestors will speak if you will hear. I have listened to the stories the old men tell. I tell them to my grandchildren, Tiana and Farrell. But they are young; they will forget. It may be that you could paint these stories. Then they would not die with me."

Asudi's soft, measured words were like a thunderbolt to Jordan. Why had he not thought of it before? He would paint Cherokee history and myth—so simple a suggestion, and yet so utterly right.

After that, he went frequently to Asudi's little cabin and listened to the old man's stories. When he began to feel truly a part of his heritage, he started to paint again. Success—as the world counts success—which had been ever out of reach before, came swiftly. Now, eight years later, his paintings had been exhibited in many large American and European cities and were a part of major collections throughout the world.

Ironically, he had helped his people more through his painting—by giving them a pride in their heritage—than he could have in a lifetime devoted to the legal profession. Although he had spent many hours with Asudi, the old storyteller, he had never told him that he, Jordan, had come to believe in Asudi's "inner voice." But Jordan had procrastinated too long. Three days ago, upon his return from two weeks in New York, a phone call had come from the attorney, George McNair, informing him that Asudi had died and been buried during his absence, and asking

7

him to come to McNair's office in Muskogee to discuss matters dealing with the old man's estate.

It seemed that Asudi had made a will, which surprised Jordan, since his friend had, in so many instances, rejected the "white man's way."

The buzzing from McNair's inner office interrupted Jordan's train of thought, and he turned toward the secretary expectantly. She spoke into the telephone, then looked up and smiled at him.

"Mr. McNair will see you now."

As Jordan opened the door, a short, heavyset man with a balding pate got up from behind a massive oak desk and came forward to pump Jordan's hand. "Sorry to keep you waiting, Mr. Ridge, but I had an unexpected long distance call."

"That's quite all right," Jordan assured him, taking one of the green leather chairs facing the desk.

McNair sat down again. "It's an honor to have you in my office, sir. I am an admirer of your work."

Jordan inclined his head. "Thank you." He was impatient to get to the purpose of the meeting. "I regret not being home when Asudi died."

"He died peacefully in his sleep, I'm told."

Jordan felt relieved to know that, at least, Asudi hadn't suffered. "I'm not sure I know why I'm here, Mr. McNair. I didn't even know that Asudi had made a will."

McNair picked up some folded papers from his desk and offered them to Jordan. "I have it here. You may read it, if you like, or I can summarize it for you."

Jordan waved the papers aside. "Just tell me, please."

"He left everything in trust for his grandchildren—Tiana and Farrell—until the boy is twenty-one. The estate consists of an eighty-acre farm, a five-room house, and a few pieces of furniture and personal belongings. Asudi named you executor of his will, Mr. Ridge. The estate will go into a trust. Fortunately, Asudi had no debts. He had one small life insurance policy that was enough to cover the funeral expenses."

Jordan relaxed against the smooth leather of the chair. "Then my job will be an easy one."

The attorney studied him for a moment before he spoke again. "There are two other stipulations. In addition to naming you executor, Asudi made you trustee and guardian of his grandson, Farrell."

Jordan sat bolt upright. "What!" He was trying to picture Asudi's grandson in his mind. He hadn't seen Farrell in some years. Most of his visits to Asudi's cabin had taken place while the boy was in school. As for the granddaughter, Tiana, Jordan hadn't seen her in an even longer time. She'd been away at college until she'd taken a job as a teacher in a Tahlequah elementary school. He became aware that McNair was watching him curiously.

"You had no idea Asudi might do this?"

Jordan shook his head, dismayed. "None. Aren't there relatives? I don't understand. Why me?"

McNair scratched his shiny pate. "The boy has no relatives except for his sister."

"She must be twenty-four or so. Why wasn't she appointed her brother's guardian?"

"Obviously Asudi trusted you to see that his grandson is properly cared for and—disciplined."

The attorney's words brought to Jordan's mind the final moments of his last visit with Asudi a month earlier. He had been about to leave; Asudi had followed him outside the cabin to say, "I'm worried about Farrell. He is rebellious and, when I try to reason with him, he calls me an old man and says I do not understand the modern world." Apparently Asudi had felt that Tiana couldn't cope with the boy.

McNair was saying, "I don't know if Tiana and Farrell want to continue living on the farm. If they intend moving to town, it will be easy to find a renter. As Farrell's guardian, you will, naturally, decide where he will live."

McNair's phone buzzed. "Yes? Good. Thank you, Mrs. McNair, I'm not married. I never even had younger brothers or sisters. What do I know about children?"

9

McNair's hazel eyes were sympathetic. "Farrell's not really a child. In fact, he'll be eighteen in October, four months from now, at which time your guardianship will end."

Great! thought Jordan harriedly. But what was he supposed to do with a seventeen-year-old boy in the meantime? He didn't know, but Asudi had left Jordan a sacred trust which his gratitude and love for the old man would not let him shirk.

McNair's phone buzzed. "Yes? Good. Thank you, Mr. Nunley." He hung up and eyed Jordan again. "They're here."

Before Jordan could reply, the office door opened and a young woman came in, followed by a slender youth of medium height. Farrell slouched just inside the office, hands thrust into the hip pockets of his tight jeans, and eyed Jordan warily from beneath shaggy black hair.

Tiana was another matter. Slender and slightly built, she held herself proudly. Clearly intending to present a businesslike manner, her alluring curves were nonetheless not completely hidden by the tailored rose-colored cotton suit she wore. A loose-fitting jacket was unbuttoned to reveal a crisp white shirt tucked into the flared skirt. Black brows arched over wide brown eyes in arresting contrast to skin of a golden tan. Thick, shining black hair was pulled back and tucked demurely into a smooth chignon. As Jordan got to his feet, he was disconcerted to find himself picturing how that hair would look unconfined, left to flow freely about Tiana's narrow shoulders and down her back.

McNair was standing behind his desk. "Tiana, Farrell, you know Mr. Ridge, don't you?"

The boy did not deign to acknowledge acquaintance with Jordan, but Tiana turned to him with a direct gaze. "Of course. At least, I feel as if I know him. He came to see my grandfather often. Hello, Jordan."

"Tiana."

"Well!" McNair was suddenly brusque. "Take that

chair, Tiana. Farrell, if you will sit beside your sister, we'll get down to business."

When everyone was seated, McNair went on. "As you know, Farrell, it was Asudi's wish that Mr. Ridge act as your guardian until your eighteenth birthday."

Farrell grumbled. "I don't need a guardian. I've got Tiana. We can get along just fine on our own."

Tiana was sitting very straight in her chair, slender hands folded in her lap. The dark eyes rested unwaveringly on Jordan's face as if she were trying to assess his reaction to the proposed guardianship.

She turned to look at the attorney, her bottom lip caught between white teeth for a moment. "There is no reason why Farrell and I can't continue living in Grandfather's cabin, as we have always done. Jordan is a busy man. He need not concern himself with my brother's welfare."

McNair replied, "I have already explained this to you, Tiana. You, of course, are free to do as you wish. But, for reasons of his own, your grandfather did not see fit to name you your brother's guardian. That responsibility, by law, belongs to Mr. Ridge."

When Tiana did not immediately respond, McNair went on. "I've already spoken to Mr. Ridge about the possibility of renting your grandfather's farm. I know a young couple who would like to move into the house right away. They would take it furnished."

Tiana stiffened as she looked from McNair to Jordan. "If we are to be moved out of our home, where are we to stay?"

McNair waited for Jordan to reply. "Tiana, I haven't had the opportunity to think this through as yet." He wished she would not look at him with betrayal in her luminous eyes. "This is something you and I and Farrell are going to have to work out between us."

McNair cleared his throat. "Good! I'm sure you'll be able to iron things out to everyone's satisfaction."

Jordan got to his feet reluctantly. "We'll not take up any more of your time, Mr. McNair."

Wordlessly, Tiana and Farrell followed Jordan from the office. In the hall outside, he looked over at them, wanting to say something to ease the tension that was in the air. Tiana was walking stiffly beside him, eyes straight ahead. On her right, Farrell, hair falling into his eyes, watched his worn canvas shoes making contact with the polished tile floor.

"It's nearly noon," Jordan said when he could stand the silence no longer. "We'll have lunch and discuss this further."

"Whatever you say," Tiana responded coldly, and Farrell gave her a murderously speaking glance.

They went to a small Chinese restaurant. "Do you like oriental food?" Jordan inquired of Farrell when they were seated.

The boy shrugged disinterestedly. "I've never tasted it." He glanced at the menu, then tossed it aside impatiently. "I don't know what any of this stuff is."

"I'll order for all of us, if that suits you, Tiana?" said Jordan, trying to stifle his own impatience. He ordered egg rolls, sweet-and-sour pork, and jasmine tea.

While they waited for the order, Jordan tried to engage Farrell in conversation. "It's about time for your school to let out for this term, isn't it?"

"I graduated last week," the boy said flatly. Glancing at Tiana, he added, "Even though my sister thought I'd never make it. Since she's a teacher, she's hung up on high grades."

Tiana's lips were pressed together in a way that suggested she had heard this complaint before.

"What do you plan to do now?" Jordan inquired.

Farrell's expression was blank. "Do? Why, I'll probably mess around this summer . . ."

Jordan eyed the boy's sullen expression and was irritated. "What do you mean by 'mess around'?"

Farrell rolled his eyes heavenward and slumped further down into his chair. "You sound like Grandfather. I don't have anything special in mind. I just want to have fun—live it up, you know?"

"Farrell has been trying to get a summer job," Tiana intervened placatingly, "but he hasn't found anything yet."

Farrell said carelessly, "They all say come back when I'm eighteen." Jordan suspected Farrell hadn't been looking very hard for employment, regardless of what he'd told his sister. The boy straightened in his chair. "Can you let me have a dollar, Tiana? I want to call some of my friends."

Tiana fished some change from her purse and, although she made no comment, Jordan sensed her disapproval. Farrell took the coins and left the table.

"You don't approve of Farrell's friends?"

Her brown eyes wavered. "I—I don't know. Farrell says I'm unfair, but some of them impress me as being irresponsible."

"Like Farrell?"

Dark eyes flew to meet his. "I didn't mean that. Farrell is young. He still has a lot of growing up to do."

"Don't you think it's time he started?"

She toyed with the spoon beside her plate. "What do you intend to do—about Farrell, I mean?"

"What do you suggest?"

"Let him stay with me in the cabin at the farm."

Jordan hated to have to oppose her so directly, but already it was fairly clear to him that she had little control over the boy. "No. I don't think that's in Farrell's best interest."

Her soft mouth became a firm, indignant line. "You know nothing about him!"

"Enough to realize that he needs to learn the meaning of discipline, if it's not already too late."

"I—I know I've probably been too lenient with him." She was obviously making an effort to remain calm and reasonable. "But he's the only family I have left. I'll talk to him, Jordan. I'll insist on certain 'house rules' and make him promise to keep them."

13

"I want him to move in with me until he's eighteen," Jordan said, unmoved by the pleading in her tone.

She was staring at him with wide brown eyes. "Do you mean you would take him away from me?"

He reached for the small hand which lay beside the folded napkin, but Tiana jerked it away. "Tiana," he said gently, "I have no intention of taking Farrell away from you. You can see him any time you want. He can come into town and visit you frequently."

"Come into town? You seem to have made a false assumption. I plan to stay at the farm until the new school term begins."

His dark brows drew together. "Is that wise?"

She pursed her lips sardonically. "I know it may be hard for someone like you to understand, but I can barely make ends meet as it is. My teaching salary is spread over nine months. I receive no checks in the summer. Last summer I took a job in a Tahlequah department store, but this year I am required to take two courses at the university to keep my certificate up-to-date. I won't be able to manage a job too. Consequently, I can't afford to rent a place in town."

His gaze swept over her lovely features—the shining hair, the delicate line of nose and chin, the slightly almond-shaped dark eyes, the pure silky texture of her golden skin—and he felt a flicker of unease at what he was about to suggest. "You are welcome to come to my house with Farrell."

Her lips were parted in astonishment, an expression that Jordan found unconsciously seductive. "You can't be serious!"

Jordan interrupted her curtly. "Before you refuse, think about it for a minute. The arrangement I suggest would allow you to rent the farm out, which would add something to your income and Farrell's. And you would be with your brother. Besides, you surely can't want to stay in that isolated cabin alone at night." The slight tremor that passed through her told Jordan he'd hit upon a touchy point. He pressed the advantage. "Did you know there

14

have been several break-ins of farm homes in Cherokee County lately?"

She nodded mutely, frowning.

"Do you have a gun?" he queried.

"No! I wouldn't know how to use one if I did—and I don't want to learn. I hate guns!"

He couldn't help smiling. "You certainly aren't strong enough to fend off a burglar barehanded." Then he sobered. "Word gets around, Tiana. It wouldn't be long before everybody in the county knew you were living out there alone."

"I wouldn't be alone," she snapped, "if you'd let Farrell—"

"Farrell moves in with me," Jordan said stubbornly.

She looked at him, her anger shining in her eyes. "When?"

"Tomorrow. Shall I tell him when he comes back to the table?"

She shook her head firmly. "No, I'll tell him later, after we get back to the farm."

"All right, if you think that's best. He might be more willing to accept the arrangement, though, if you would come with him. You can let me know tomorrow what you've decided. Oh, here's our food, and Farrell is coming this way too."

They ate their meal in silence after Jordan made a few abortive attempts at conversation with Farrell. The boy was clearly on the defensive.

When they left the restaurant, Jordan said, "I expect I'll be seeing the two of you soon." He sent Tiana a conspiratorial look.

Her return glance was scathing. "Thank you for lunch."

"I told the guys," Farrell said to his sister, "I could probably use your car tonight, Tiana."

"Good afternoon, Jordan," Tiana said, turning away. "Come along, Farrell. You shouldn't make plans which include the use of my car without first consulting me."

As they walked away from Jordan, Farrell's wheedling

tones reached back to him. Clearly, Farrell was accustomed to getting around whatever objections his sister might offer.

Jordan walked a block in the opposite direction, got into his midnight-blue Jaguar, and roared away. Brooding over the unavoidable changes in his life which Asudi's will was bringing about, he reached the highway leading out of the city. He felt Asudi would approve of the arrangements Jordan had made for his grandson. Would he also approve of his beautiful granddaughter living in Jordan's house? After all, Jordan's housekeeper, Millie Carver, a half-Choctaw woman, was in the house five days a week, but she went back to her home in town evenings and on weekends.

Jordan's artist imagination insisted on seeing again the silky swathe of Tiana's black hair spilling down her back and the unconscious grace with which she moved. If she came, he told himself, it would only be for three months. Perhaps they wouldn't get in each other's way for that length of time—plenty of time, nevertheless, for gossip to get around. Not that he cared much for the opinions of others, but Asudi wouldn't have liked people gossiping about Tiana. Since bringing her and Farrell to live with him after their parents were killed in a car crash several years earlier, the old storyteller had been fiercely protective of them both.

Jordan continued to brood until he reached the small university town of Tahlequah, which was only about twenty-five miles from his country place. On a sudden impulse, he parked in front of The Toadstool, Lois Graham's chic dress shop. He'd been seeing Lois, off and on, for almost two years.

A twenty-eight-year-old divorcee, Lois had made it abundantly clear that she would like to be Mrs. Jordan Ridge. Jordan had tried to make it as clear to her that he had no intention of marrying anyone. He was a diehard bachelor. Not that he didn't enjoy women tremendously on a temporary basis. He smiled to himself and, shrugging off his momentary hesitation, he climbed out of the car. Lois knew where he stood, so there was no reason to feel guilty.

The shop was empty of customers when he entered. Lois looked up from a rack of dresses she was tagging and smiled warmly. "Jordan! Why didn't you let me know you'd be in town today?" She came toward him, moving with that consciously provocative swing of her hips, and lifted her face to brush his hard cheek with her lips.

"You are so naughty, Jordan," she said in a low, husky voice, "not to let me know you were coming. I'm here alone for the rest of the day."

He smiled at her in a rather absentminded way and patted her hand. "I didn't plan it. I had to go to Muskogee on business and only stopped on impulse."

She fluttered her heavily mascaraed lashes at him. "I do love your impulses, Jordan!"

He laughed good-naturedly, unable to stifle a fleeting comparison between Lois's artificial, made-up look and Tiana's delightfully natural beauty. "Maybe you can spare a weary traveler a cup of coffee."

"You bet I can, honey! Come on back to my office. I've got a fresh pot. We'll hear the bell if anyone comes in."

Lois's office, fussily decorated in pink and white, looked more like a boudoir than a place of business. Ordinarily, Jordan found the room ridiculously funny. At present, though, he hardly felt amused. He flopped into one of the armless pink velvet chairs, stretching his long legs out across the white carpet, and heard the thing creak warningly. "I'm going to break one of your chairs some day," he grumbled.

Lois was pouring coffee from an electric percolator into two dainty china cups on the small, organdy-covered table in one corner. "I don't entertain many men back here," she returned coyly. "This is a ladies' shop, honey." She carried his cup to him and sat down on the chaise longue near him.

Jordan drained the small cup in three good swallows,

17

then set it on the floor, put his head back against the up-holstered chair cushion, and closed his eyes.

He was half asleep when Lois's sulky voice brought him back to reality.

"What's wrong, honey?"

He hadn't meant to tell her, but since she was there and he had to tell someone, he described the salient aspects of his afternoon briefly.

When he finished, she laughed. "Oh, Jordan, I can't imagine you playing daddy to a teenage boy!"

He hadn't mentioned the possibility that Tiana, also, might become a part of his household. He scowled. "I felt like a heel insisting the kid move in with me. Yet I know it's what the old man would want."

"Well, sweetie, what else could you have done?" Lois inquired reasonably as she laid a cheek against his leg.

"I'm supposed to pick him up tomorrow. I guess I'll have to learn what teenagers these days enjoy if I'm to get close to him at all."

"Oh, shoot," said Lois, her full lips pouting, "I guess I'll see even less of you now. When you aren't chumming with your ward, I suppose you'll be working on some old paint-ings for that silly Paris exhibition in the fall."

Jordan chuckled. "Lois, you're the only person I know who would call an exhibition in one of Paris's most presti-gious museums silly."

She lifted her cheek from his leg, brightening suddenly. "I have a wonderful idea. I'll close the shop early, and we'll go to my place. I bought a couple of T-bones yester-day, and I have an unopened bottle of Chablis."

This was exactly the sort of scene Jordan had been pic-turing when he decided to stop at the shop. Now that it was offered to him, however, he felt a perverse desire to get away from Lois.

"I can't stay," he heard himself saying. "I have to work tonight."

As he stood, so did she. "Work, work, work! That's all you think about, Jordan."

He pulled her to him and kissed her thoroughly. "Not all," he said with a twinkle in his eye. She moved closer to him, but he stepped back. "Put those steaks in the freezer. We'll have them soon."

"What about Saturday?"

"I'll try."

She smiled seductively. "Try hard, honey."

He gave her a playful swat on the bottom and left the shop. Four miles from his house he turned off the highway onto a winding graveled road. The stone-and-cedar tri-level house, which he'd built five years ago on a newly acquired hundred-and-sixty wooded acres, was not visible from the road, and that was just as Jordan had planned it. He enjoyed his isolation when he was painting. Fortunately, his housekeeper wasn't a compulsive talker, although she could speak her piece when the occasion demanded.

He turned into his drive, marked by a silver-colored mailbox, circled the house, and parked in the garage in back next to the jeep he used for traveling about the farm.

He bounded up the steps to the cedar deck, stripping off jacket and tie as he went. Millie had already gone home, but she'd left a roast in the warm oven. He made a thick roast beef sandwich and poured a tall glass of iced tea, taking them out to the deck where he settled into one of the canvas deck chairs.

Duke, his collie, returned from hunting rabbits in the woods and, ecstatic at discovering his master was at home, leaped onto the deck and laid his head on Jordan's lap. Absently, Jordan scratched the collie's ears, eliciting grunts of satisfaction.

He had intended to work awhile before going to bed, but he found himself unable to concentrate on painting. Instead, he sat on the deck with Duke until very late, and it was nearly midnight when he finally went to bed.

2

Tiana stood in the verdant stillness that had calmed even the crickets and lulled them into silence. All around her the dark woods seemed to be holding its breath; and then, from far away, came the yipping of a coyote. The sound released the crickets from their spell, and they began droning again. Farrell had not yet returned from Tahlequah. Restlessly, Tiana paced back and forth on the porch of the cabin. Tonight her worries could not be dissipated by talking to her grandfather; Asudi was gone.

Had he been here, she knew what he would have said: *Be calm, Tiana. Worry never changed anything. Whatever happens will happen.* With resolution, she ceased pacing and entered the cabin. She sat in a creaking rocker by the front window.

She should have refused to give Farrell her car, but she had crumpled in the face of his wheedling, as she usually did. She had not found a good time to tell her brother that he would be moving in with Jordan Ridge the next day and, after dinner, when he had started in on her about the car, she had welcomed the few hours' delay his absence would provide. Now she wished she had told him earlier; perhaps then she would be able to push the vague worries about Farrell's welfare to the back of her mind and sleep.

She rested her head against the high back of the rocker and closed her eyes. She saw again the dark, brooding face of Jordan Ridge, hardened by the stubborn set of his jaw as he told her he wanted Farrell to move in with him and suggested she come and stay with her brother. She had had several hours now to think about that suggestion.

Although she had wrestled the arguments back and forth in her mind repeatedly, her decision had probably been made—subconsciously—before she and Farrell parted from Jordan in Muskogee. Farrell was all she had left in the world, and, if she wanted to keep him with her, she would have to accept Jordan's hospitality.

She resented Jordan for being given the responsibility that should have been hers, even though she understood Asudi's reasons for making his will as he had. She was objective enough to know that she had little real authority over her brother. Ever since their parents were killed when he was five and Tiana twelve, he had been able to whine and coax her into agreeing to almost anything. Until the past year this hadn't worked so decidedly against Farrell, for their grandfather had been there to put his foot down when he felt things were going too far. During the last year, however, Asudi had lost the vigor and indomitable will that had always been so much a part of him. Toward the last, she had suspected—as his subsequent death had proved—that he was feeling too ill to exercise his authority as head of the family.

Now, as she thought about spending the summer in the same house with Jordan Ridge, Tiana shivered and pulled her bare legs up in the chair, tucking the skirt of her cotton nightgown around them. The first time she had seen him was about five years ago. She had been home from college for spring vacation and, during a long ramble through the woods, had happened onto his property. She found herself at the edge of the woods atop a small hill that looked down on the new stone-and-cedar house that accommodated itself to the contours of the land so well that it looked as if it had been there for years.

As soon as she caught sight of the house, she had known where she was. Her grandfather had mentioned a few months before that his friend, Jordan Ridge, the painter, had bought land near Asudi's and was building a house.

Tiana had stayed hidden in the cover of the trees, looking down at the house until Jordan had come out onto the deck, carrying an easel. He had been wearing only faded blue swimming trunks, and she had watched, fascinated, as he set up the easel, brought his paints and brushes out, and started to paint, occasionally gazing out over the woodsy countryside with an expression of total absorption.

During the next couple of years, she had walked to that hillside whenever she was home from college and, several times, had found Jordan at work on the deck. She had watched him in that setting so many times that, when she had walked into George McNair's office to see him sitting there in suit and tie, it had come as something of a shock and she had had to fight off a sense of fantasy as if none of it was quite real.

The fact that she had not walked onto Jordan's property for the previous three years added to the feeling of unreality. During the past two years she had been teaching the second grade in Tahlequah and, even though she continued to live with Asudi and Farrell on the farm, grading papers and other teaching chores had taken up much of her time at home. The year before that—her senior year at the university—there had been Edward. . . .

Even after all this time, she still could not think of Edward Shipman without a painful constriction in her chest, a feeling that was a mixture of heartbreak, wounded pride, and iron determination never to be so vulnerable again.

As a teenager, Tiana had been painfully shy. Added to that, the fact that she lived in the country away from her classmates made it difficult for her to make friends. Consequently, she had not dated many boys. Later, at the university, she had continued her solitary way of life, making a few close girl friends and spending her evenings and weekends buried in her studies. Then, at the beginning of her senior year, she had met Edward, a gregarious, self-confident, auburn-haired young man who was everything Tiana admired. He had pursued her persistently until he broke through the barrier of her shyness and she had agreed to go out with him. They had dated steadily all year and, in April, become engaged, planning to marry the following autumn.

Edward went to Nebraska to work for the summer and Tiana found a job in Tahlequah so that they could save money to set up housekeeping. Edward's letters were infrequent, but he explained that he was working long hours and was usually too tired after the day's work to write. Tiana accepted this explanation without a second thought and continued her thrice-weekly letters to him filled with how much she missed him and how eagerly she looked forward to his return.

Edward's last letter had come during the final week of August. Tiana could still close her eyes and bring that hot summer day back as if it were yesterday.

Seeing Edward's neat handwriting on the envelope in the box, she had felt her heart leap joyously and, without waiting to get back to the cabin, she had opened it. The words were burned into her memory: "Tiana, I've been trying to write this letter for a month and now that summer is almost over I can't put it off any longer. I won't be coming back to Oklahoma. I've met a girl here and we are getting married in a couple of weeks. I don't know how it happened, Tiana. I honestly thought I loved you—until I met Marie and then I realized I'd never really known what love was all about. I don't know what else to say except I'm sorry. I never meant to hurt you. . . ."

She had spent the next two days locked in her bedroom, nursing the hurt and wishing that she could die. Fortunately for her sanity, she had signed a teaching contract and, on the last day of August, she was forced to get dressed and go into town to begin the school year. The job which she had seen as a stopgap measure until she and Edward decided to have a family became her salvation. She became the most dedicated teacher in the Tahlequah school system.

Only in recent months had she begun to go out again, with the vice-principal of her school, Dale Gregory—and

24

only after she was sure their relationship could be based on warm affection between equals, in no way akin to the naive, adoring hero-worship she had felt for Edward.

During those two desolate days in her bedroom, after reading Edward's last letter, resolve had hardened in her like concrete—resolve never to lay herself open to such pain again. The one time she had overcome her shyness and reserve and given her heart, it had been thrown back in her face. Never did she intend to be hurt like that again.

She had become independent and self-sufficient, allowing herself only one outlet for deep emotion—the love and indulgence she showered on her brother, Farrell. Perhaps that was why she could never seem to say no to him, even when she knew that she ought to.

It was also why she would go to live in Jordan's house; she could not bear to be separated from the only person she allowed herself to love without reservation.

She would rent the farm and put the money away for Farrell when he came to legal age. Somehow she would pay their way in Jordan's house. She knew that he had a housekeeper, but she would make herself useful to the woman. She didn't care how wealthy the Cherokee painter might be, she had no intention of becoming obligated to him.

Their meeting in the attorney's office had impressed upon her anew an uncomfortable truth: Jordan Ridge was the sort of supremely masculine man that some women found irresistible. Indeed, if the stories of his conquests were to be believed, he used his sex appeal mercilessly. Tiana was determined not to fall prey to that appeal. She had spent the past two years building emotional defenses, and she had built carefully and well. She had no doubt that this would carry her through the next few months unscathed.

When autumn came and Farrell turned eighteen, she would find a place for the two of them in town.

The soft breeze that was stirring the white curtains at the window was growing cooler. As if to underscore the recent changes in her life, thunder rolled in the distance. Instead of troubling her, however, the sound brought a trembling smile to her lips. The old Cherokees had always looked upon the thunder as a friend, even a guardian presence. Her grandfather had told many stories in which Thunder came to man's aid. Remembering Asudi's stories made him seem closer and gave Tiana renewed courage to face the unwanted change of residence with confidence.

Finally, she gave up her vigil and went to bed. The emotional upheaval of the day soon weighed heavily upon her eyelids. She drifted into sleep, only half-rousing when Farrell came in after midnight. Vaguely, she heard him stumble into a piece of furniture in the living room and wondered fleetingly if he had been drinking again. But she was too sleepy to get up and confront him. Tomorrow would be time enough, she thought, and that was Jordan's responsibility now. Somehow relieved by this, she went back to sleep.

She awoke before eight and was packing Farrell's clothes into a cardboard box when he shuffled, yawning and swollen-eyed, into the kitchen.

"Cinnamon rolls in the oven," she told him.

Mumbling sleepily, he poured himself a glass of milk and carried the platter of rolls to the small kitchen table, where he dropped into a chair. Through the open door to the living room, his gaze fell on Tiana.

"What're you doing?"

"Packing your things. We're moving in with Jordan Ridge this afternoon."

The slumped form bolted upright in the kitchen chair. *"What?"*

"That's right," said Tiana, maintaining a calm exterior. "Your guardian has decided it's what you ought to do. I'm going along so that we won't have to be separated."

"I won't move in with him!"

Tiana laid the last pair of folded jeans into the box and came to stand in the kitchen doorway. "Please don't be difficult, Farrell. Jordan won't change his mind. I've al-

26

ready tried to talk to him. All we can do is make the best of things, and it will only be for four months."

Farrell had gotten to his feet and was pacing furiously about the kitchen now. "Well, he can't make me!"

"Yes, he can. If you refuse, he can turn your guardianship over to the court. They would send you to a foster home which would probably be much worse than living with Jordan. Don't try to defy him, Farrell. It won't work."

Farrell muttered a curse. "Grandfather sure messed up everything with that nutty will."

"He did what he thought was best. Come on, try to look on the bright side. You'll have your own bedroom in that beautiful house. You'll have the run of the grounds, and his private lake for swimming. I think he even keeps some horses for riding. The summer will pass quickly. You'll see." She tried a cajoling smile. "You might even start to enjoy it."

"Not likely!"

In spite of Farrell's strong aversion to the idea of living with Jordan, he did eventually agree, albeit with sullen reluctance.

Jordan came for them in his jeep, which Farrell eyed with disappointment. "I heard you had a Jag."

"I do," Jordan told him, "but this has more room for your things." He helped Farrell carry the suitcases and boxes to the jeep where they stowed them in back. Noticing a pair of woman's sandals in one box, he said to Tiana, "You've decided to come too? I think that's the most sensible thing for everyone."

Standing next to him, Tiana realized, as she had yesterday, that she hadn't forgotten a detail of his appearance since the days when she watched him secretly from the woods—dark features, high cheekbones with faint hollows beneath, black hair that riffled softly in the breeze. The narrowed eyes that held hers were as dark brown and intense as she remembered, fixing her with a look that tautened her nerves. Sensible? She was not at all sure that

27

word correctly described her decision to move into Jordan's house.

Unexpectedly, Tiana's throat had gone dry and she dropped her gaze to the red knit shirt Jordan wore tucked into denim pants that hugged his long, powerful legs. Yesterday he had worn a handsomely tailored suit and his proud carriage and stern insistence on planning Farrell's future had made her feel inadequate, like an irresponsible babysitter who had let Farrell run wild. But right now he made her conscious of herself as a woman and the feeling was even more alarming.

"Are we ready?" His fingers had descended casually on her shoulder and their strong grip sent a tingle all the way down her arm. Tiana pulled back nervously, and his sardonic glance informed her that he was aware of his own sexual attraction.

"Farrell can go with you and I'll follow in my car," she said abruptly. When she cast another quick look at him she found his eyes fixed on her mouth. Uneasily, she fingered the collar of her shirt as she turned away and headed for her car. It infuriated her that, in spite of her aversion to his way of life, he could nevertheless make her aware of him as a man.

For a moment, when she glanced over her shoulder, she saw Farrell standing hesitantly beside the jeep, his eyes following her. She had the feeling he wanted to refuse to ride with Jordan. As she watched, Jordan said something abruptly, then climbed into the driver's seat, and Farrell got in without a word.

When they reached Jordan's house and had been introduced to Millie Carver, she led them along a hall in the lowest level to their bedrooms.

"It'll be good for Jordan to have the two of you around," Millie told them. "He spends too much time alone."

Thinking of Jordan's women friends, Tiana bit back a sarcastic disclaimer. She was, at least, relieved to discover that the artist's bedroom was next to his studio on the third level at the opposite end of the house.

Each of the guest bedrooms was large and had many windows and its own bath. Farrell's room was suitably masculine, with a brown shag carpet, heavy maple furniture, and bedspread and draperies of a loosely woven coffee-colored fabric.

Tiana's room was decorated in shades of blue with a brass bed, royal blue carpet, and bedspread and draperies of a blue floral cotton material. Sliding glass doors in one wall opened onto the redwood deck that wrapped itself around three sides of the house.

As soon as the housekeeper left them alone, Farrell flopped down on his bed, his bottom lip pushed out in a pout. Ignoring him, Tiana began hanging his clothes up in his closet. When she had finished, she left him alone to go to her own bedroom. Her classes at Northeastern State in Tahlequah started on Monday and, this being Friday, she wanted to be comfortably settled in by the beginning of the week.

She did not see Jordan again until he came out of his studio for dinner. By that time Tiana and Millie were on a first-name basis, Tiana having insisted on helping with the meal preparation. Farrell had made friends with Duke, the collie, and spent the afternoon exploring Jordan's property with the dog at his heels.

They ate dinner at a table next to the glassed-in section of the huge living area that, with the kitchen and utility room, occupied the middle level of the house. The size of the room was emphasized by a tall, beamed ceiling, a massive stone fireplace on the east wall, and an oversized beige leather pit sofa arranged in a U facing the fireplace. The focal point of the room, however, was a large watercolor that hung over the fireplace. It depicted the Cherokees on the Trail of Tears, their bent, blanket-wrapped bodies starkly tragic against a background of blue-white snow. It was one of Jordan's best-known works, often exhibited, done, like much of his early work, in the somewhat two-dimensional traditional Indian style. Tiana had seen it a number of times in shows but, like all good paintings, one never grew tired of studying it. Surprisingly, it was the only example of Jordan's work in evidence.

Their table overlooked the redwood deck and the wooded hillside beyond. Farrell was still uncommunicative, responding tersely to Jordan's questions about his afternoon. Tiana was relieved when the meal was over; she helped Millie clean up the kitchen before the housekeeper left for her house in town.

As Millie was leaving, Tiana, who was still in the kitchen, heard Jordan say, "Would you mind making a phone call for me when you get home? Call Lois Graham and cancel our date for tomorrow night. Tell her I'll be in to see her next week and explain."

Then Tiana heard the door closing behind Millie and, suddenly, the house seemed very quiet. She looked out the kitchen window and saw Farrell sitting on the deck with Duke by his side. She knew he was still feeling resentment, but she hoped that after a few days his attitude would soften.

"Any coffee left?"

The unexpected deep voice in the silence caused Tiana to jump as she turned to see Jordan standing in the kitchen doorway. "No, but I could make some instant."

"Would you mind? Then if you'll join me in the living room, I'd like to talk to you."

A few minutes later Tiana carried two mugs of coffee into the living room. She handed one to Jordan, who was sprawled on the leather sofa, and sat down, leaving the space of a cushion between them. She had changed into slacks and a pink silk blouse before dinner. Jordan was wearing the same red knit shirt and denim pants he'd had on earlier in the day. His thick black hair fell loosely to his collar in a style which—although much neater than Farrell's longer, unshaped locks—she thought untidy.

In spite of the relaxed attitude of his appearance and posture, however, there was something darkly intense in this man—an electric sort of drive which undoubtedly accounted for his enormous success as a painter. Her glance flicked involuntarily to his mouth, which was a little too wide, the top lip firm and controlled, the lower fuller, with a hint of sensuality. She sat straight, knees primly together, and, as he sipped his coffee, Tiana's hand went, in an unconscious and unnecessary gesture, to smooth her chignon.

He lowered his cup, his dark eyes surveying her, a derisive tilt to one corner of his mouth. "Are you always so neat?"

Something in his tone brought a warmth to her face, a discomfort that did not show in the golden tan of her complexion but which made itself known in the tight pressing together of her lips. "I—I try to be. I think teachers should be."

"Oh!" he said, a slightly teasing gleam in the dark eyes. "Well, you're not in the classroom now. I want you to feel at home here, Tiana. Let your hair down, wear jeans—do whatever you are accustomed to doing at home."

Her eyes sparked with irritation. "But this isn't my home. It's only a place where I am forced to stay temporarily, or be separated from my brother." She gazed at the slender hands which were curled around the coffee mug in her lap.

He spoke with dry emphasis. "You won't help Farrell with that attitude." She looked up again and their eyes met. She felt a shivery sensation run down her spine, as though he had touched her.

"Have you made any arrangements for the weekend?" he queried abruptly.

Her eyes widened. "What I do with my time is none of your concern. Perhaps I should remind you that you are Farrell's guardian, not mine."

"It's because of Farrell that I ask the question," he retorted scornfully. "I plan to stay at home all weekend, and I think you should do the same. We could arrange some activities for the three of us—maybe a picnic tomorrow and a swim in the lake. I want Farrell to get to know me under the best possible circumstances."

31

Sighing, she said, "All right. I did have plans for Saturday evening, but I'll cancel them. Dale will understand."

"Dale?"

Something in the amused tone irked her. Her eyes hardened. "Dale Gregory. He's the vice-principal of my school." Then she halted, wondering why she should be explaining this to Jordan and what right he had to question her about it in the first place. She added in uncharacteristic confusion, "He's very understanding."

"How convenient," he said sardonically. "Then he won't lift an eyebrow at your moving in here?"

"Why should he?" she said in defiance, her chin lifting. "Dale trusts me."

"Are you engaged to him?"

Tiana's face tightened with anger. "Neither of us wants to rush into anything."

"I presume," he retorted with a wicked grin, "that includes bed."

The words took her breath away. Gripping her coffee mug, she said furiously, "How dare you make such a personal remark to me!"

Abruptly, he set his mug aside and was leaning toward her, only a few inches separating their faces. All of this happened before she was even aware that he had moved. Looking fixedly into her eyes, he said, "I'd raise the roof over your living in another man's house, if you were my woman."

Her lips curled scornfully. "Just because you jump into bed with anyone in sight, that doesn't mean everybody does. And, to set the record straight, I am nobody's woman, as you so quaintly put it, except my own."

Insolently, he moved a hand to the stray wisp of hair which had, so uncharacteristically, escaped her chignon and fallen across one cheek. Slowly he lifted it, curling it idly about his finger. "What's this? A stray lock? How wanton."

She shifted, leaning back in the angle of the sofa, effectively pulling the bit of hair from his grasp. With trembling hands she lifted her mug and sipped the nearly cold coffee.

"I don't suppose if I asked you to take your hair down you'd do it?" he asked with a teasing tilt of black brows.

Flustered, she said tightly, "No, I wouldn't."

He grinned. "What if I said my interest in seeing you in such a disheveled state was purely professional?"

Belatedly, she tucked the stray wisp of hair into place. "I wouldn't believe you."

"Ah," he returned with mock chagrin, "I perceive that you do not trust me, Tiana."

"Not an inch," she said bitterly. She set her coffee mug on the table next to the sofa and faced him determinedly. "Let us understand one another, Jordan. I am here to be with Farrell. Since this is your house and I am here only so long as your hospitality holds, I will try to be civil to you. I'd prefer it if you'd give me some work to do around here by which I could repay you for Farrell's and my room and board. I have no desire to be beholden to you."

"Very wise," he said, tongue in cheek. "Otherwise, I might demand something in exchange which you're not prepared to give." His gaze focused on her mouth disturbingly. "I'm sure you'd prefer scrubbing floors. Too bad you find me so resistible."

Grimly, she said, "I regret being the one to bruise your ego."

He smiled tantalizingly. "I think I can survive the summer on your terms—if you insist—but can you, Tiana?"

The softly caressing way he said her name made her tingle with alarm. "Perfectly well." They stared at each other in the silence that followed. Tiana could hear the sound of her heart beating in her ears. Shakily, she said, "If you will excuse me now, I'll go out and join Farrell on the deck."

"Good night, Tiana," he said curtly.

3

Tiana turned from tucking a checked cloth about the edges of the picnic basket. "Try to forget that you don't like Jordan and have a good time this afternoon, Farrell."

Her brother slouched against the door frame separating the kitchen from a small hall and watched her with broodingly resentful eyes. "Oh, I bet we have a blast," Farrell said with heavy sarcasm. "You and me and Jordan Ridge. Just one happy little family."

"That may be exaggerating things a bit," Tiana replied with a smile, "but do try to be civil."

Farrell tossed black hair from his eyes. "It's hard to be friendly with him when he's already told me I can't go into town this weekend. I'd made plans with my friends to go to a drive-in movie tonight. What am I supposed to tell them? My *guardian* won't let me go?"

Absently, Tiana tucked her cotton shirt into the waistband of her jeans. Because of the swimsuit she was wearing underneath, it kept slipping out. "He wants the three of us to get acquainted this weekend," she said patiently, lifting the picnic basket from the table and swinging it forward in both hands. "Tell them that—and carry this for me."

Farrell took the basket with a sullen pout. "There will be other weekends," Tiana continued coaxingly. "Do you have your swimming trunks?"

"I've got them on under my jeans," he said and left the kitchen.

Jordan and Duke met them in the front yard where Jordan had been clipping the holly hedge along the east side of the porch. He was wearing a faded denim shirt, which he had not bothered to button in front, tan swimming trunks, and worn canvas deck shoes. "Ready?" This, with a measuring glance past Tiana at Farrell, who stood several steps behind.

Farrell ignored Jordan, turning to pat the collie, who had bounded to his side and was sniffing at the picnic basket. Farrell held the basket aloft and started around the house with Duke, tongue lolling out greedily, at his heels.

"He's crazy about fried chicken," Jordan explained.

"I made enough for everybody, including Duke," Tiana replied brightly, determined to make the afternoon's outing friendly in spite of Farrell's belligerence. He just needed time to get used to the new set-up. Jordan's idea to spend the weekend together was a good one, she admitted somewhat reluctantly. Personally, she would have preferred not being thrown so closely with Jordan, but it seemed to be the only way that Farrell could be brought to accept his guardianship.

Jordan said, "I'll go get some towels."

"I put a couple in the picnic basket," Tiana told him.

He smiled faintly and, with a light touch at the small of her back, guided her out of the yard in a direction other than the one Farrell had taken. "This route to the lake is a little shorter," he said. He let his hand drop and walked languidly beside her.

Feeling called upon to make conversation, Tiana said in a rush, "I left the soft drink bottles in the freezer for a couple of hours, so they should be about right for drinking when we're ready to eat. And I packed ice in plastic bags around the potato salad. It's not good to let it get warm before you eat it, you know. The fried pies would have been better warm but—" She paused uncertainly, noticing that Jordan was looking at her with amusement. "I guess you can't have everything," she finished lamely.

"On the contrary," he said, straight-faced. "You seem to have made provision for all contingencies. What time did you get up this morning?"

"Six," she said defensively. "To make the fried pies. I'm not used to your kitchen and I wanted to allow plenty of time. When I do something, I like to do it right." Belatedly, she realized that this last remark sounded rather smug.

"Commendable," murmured Jordan with a sardonic lift of black brows. "You seem to be the epitome of the proper spinster schoolmarm. A place for everything and everything in its place. I'll bet your students have to sit in straight rows and raise their hands for permission to leave their seats."

Tiana felt the warmth rising in her cheeks. "There is no need for you to be condescending, Jordan," she said stiffly. "I don't feel called upon to apologize because I have discipline in my classes and demand respect from my students." She glanced at him and caught a devilish glint in his eyes. "I get it too," she added hotly.

"I don't doubt that," returned Jordan promptly. "Which makes me wonder why you haven't imposed some of that discipline on Farrell."

"You have made it abundantly clear that you disapprove of the way I handle Farrell," she retorted, fighting to remain calm. "But it's different when the child is your brother. If I've erred, it was on the side of love."

Jordan sighed disparagingly. "Love! That's a cop-out, Tiana. It usually is. People use love as an excuse for all kinds of stupid and irrational behavior."

She wondered at the bitter edge to the words. Had he been hurt by love at some time in the past? This thought was quickly discarded. If anyone had been hurt, it had been the women that Jordan Ridge took up and tossed aside with such regularity. Perhaps it was merely his oblique way of telling her that whatever ideas she might have gotten from his insinuating words and behavior the previous evening, love had no place in his life. Well, that was fine with her! She had loved without reservation once—and once was quite enough! Nor was she willing to settle for some tawdry little affair which might add a bit of spice to the great painter's summer.

They had entered the wood that stood between the house and the lake. "Regardless of what you think of Farrell's upbringing thus far," she said as she bent to pass beneath a low tree branch, "I think you're being unreasonable to forbid his going out with his friends tonight."

Jordan had stopped ahead of her and was holding a branch aside so that she could follow the path without becoming entangled. "Do you?" he asked thinly.

"Yes," she said as she passed him without meeting his gaze. "Surely you don't mean to deny him friends."

Jordan caught up with her where the path widened, falling into step beside her. "I talked to Farrell about his friends this morning while you were in the kitchen. It was like pulling teeth, I might add, but after I got a few names I went to my bedroom and called Ben Arnold to ask what he knew about them."

Tiana stopped short and stared up at him. "You called the superintendent of schools?"

Jordan shrugged. "He happens to be an old friend of mine. I didn't mention Farrell's name if that's what's worrying you. According to Ben, the boys Farrell associates with are a pretty wild bunch. Rebellious toward authority and shiftless were the terms Ben used. Did you know that Farrell has been involved in at least one chicken race out on the old highway south of town?"

"Chicken race?" she said blankly. "What's that?"

Jordan started walking again and she had to run to catch up and hear his response. "Two cars are positioned at opposite ends of a stretch of straight highway and when someone gives the signal the drivers take off down the center of the road toward each other, gas pedals to the floor. The first one to swerve aside to avoid a collision is a chicken."

Tiana felt a cold finger of dread invade her chest.

"Ben had it on pretty good authority," Jordan went on calmly. "It's possible that Farrell wasn't driving one of the cars, but he was there. If he continues to associate with boys like that, it's only a matter of time until—"

"Good Lord!" Tiana cut in explosively. "I can't believe Farrell would be a part of something so dangerous. I'll talk to him. He has to understand that he's flirting with disaster."

"They'd probably been drinking," Jordan said slowly, and the way he said it told her he meant definitely, not probably. "I'd rather you'd leave that talk to me. I don't want to unload everything on him at once, but we're going to have to establish some rules as to where he goes and with whom."

Tiana ran her tongue over lips that were suddenly dry. "Maybe if he didn't have so much time on his hands—"

"I've been considering how to remedy that." He did not elaborate further and, while one part of her was relieved to have somebody take Farrell in hand, another part resented his high-handed manner. Apparently he saw no reason to consult her about anything concerning Farrell. It was so typically arrogant of the man that she had to fight hard not to retort angrily. No small portion of her indignation was due to the fact that Jordan, after less than twenty-four hours as Farrell's guardian, had learned something about his activities that Tiana, who had spent more than seventeen years with him, had not even dreamed of.

They came out of the woods at the edge of the small lake. Farrell and Duke were already playing together in the water, Farrell tossing a small stick to the bank where Duke, barking exuberantly, would retrieve it. The picnic basket was resting well above the ground in the crotch of a big elm tree.

"By the way," said Jordan casually, coming up beside her. "I like your hair down."

Tiana fingered the ribbon at the nape of her neck which held her long hair away from her face. She hoped Jordan didn't think his request of the previous evening had anything to do with her not putting her hair up today. "It's the best way for swimming," she said quickly.

"Of course," he agreed, a teasing gleam in the brown depths of his eyes. "I certainly didn't imagine you did it for my benefit." Abruptly, he stepped out of his shoes and shucked the denim shirt. The midday sun fell on the broad expanse of his chest and shoulders, giving his skin a deep bronze glow. Involuntarily, Tiana's eyes were drawn to the flat muscles of his stomach. She looked away quickly, but not before Jordan had noticed the direction of her gaze and grinned.

"Let's swim before we eat," he said. He walked to the deep end of the lake and dove in, leaving Tiana to strip down to her lime-green maillot and follow.

She stepped to the grassy bank on the shallow edge of the lake and waded in, shivering a little. In spite of the hot June sun, the water was still bracingly cold. She swam briskly to Farrell's side, getting her blood circulating warmly, and joined him in playing with Duke. Across the lake, Jordan swam vigorously back and forth, seemingly oblivious to any presence but his own.

After a while, Tiana and Farrell climbed up the grassy bank and flopped down, panting. Duke, who was standing nearby, decided to shake himself free of some of the water streaming from his coat. Tiana jumped up, squealing, "Duke! Stop that!"

The collie ducked his head and backed away. Farrell came immediately to his aid. "It's okay, boy." Giving Tiana a disgusted look, he added, "He didn't know he was getting water on you."

Tiana shook her head and sat back down on the grass. That dog had certainly found a champion in Farrell. There was at least one thing at Jordan's that Farrell didn't resent, and this gave Tiana a small glimmer of hope. Duke's feelings having been soothed, boy and dog were now stretched out on the grass near her.

Jordan sat down beside Tiana, tossing a towel in her direction. "Sit on that and you won't get grass all over you."

She spread the towel flat and stretched out on her back. "You didn't swim long," she said.

He sat with legs drawn up, his arms encircling them

loosely. "I swam hard, though. It's great exercise. I swam almost every day last summer. I used to get up at dawn and come down here and swim and think about whatever painting I was working on at the time. There's something about swimming that frees the creative juices."

Tiana's arm rested on her forehead, shading her eyes as she looked up at the man sitting beside her. When he spoke of his work, a new tone had crept into his voice—something compounded of eagerness and reverence. Whatever might be said of Jordan Ridge in other areas, his painting touched the deep places in people, undoubtedly because it came from deep within himself. Tiana had been enormously moved by some of his paintings. They made her feel humble in the face of such talent and enormously proud of her Cherokee heritage as well. She wondered now how such a superbly empathic artist could be so hard, even cruel, in his private life.

"Every time I come here," he was saying now, "I think of that story Asudi used to tell about that friend of his younger days who saw the Little People in a lake."

"It's been years since I heard Grandfather tell that story," Tiana said. "Once I asked him where that lake was, and he said his friend had died before he could ask him."

Jordan chuckled. "He told me the same thing. But I've often wondered if this could be the lake."

Farrell spoke suddenly, almost accusingly. "I don't remember any story like that."

"Let's see if I can remember it," Jordan said slowly, gazing out over the lake through narrowed eyes. "It seems this friend of Asudi's got lost while walking home one night. In his wandering about, searching for the road, he found himself at the edge of a lake. There was a full moon that night, and he looked into the water and saw some Little People and a house deep down at the bottom of the lake."

"Then he looked up and saw a door in the bank," Tiana put in, delighted that Jordan was recalling a memory that had been almost lost.

"That's right," Jordan agreed, "and he went through the

41

door and discovered that he was in the place he had seen from the bank. He talked with the Little People and ate with them." A faint smile played about his wide mouth. "They gave him raccoon meat, as I recall. After the meal, the Little People danced all night while Asudi's friend watched. In the morning, he left by the door in the bank." Jordan paused then, as if trying to recall how Asudi had ended the tale.

"After he had walked a short distance," Tiana provided, "he looked back and could not see the door. It had disappeared."

Jordan gave her an appreciative glance. "I'm going to do a painting of the Little People. The old Cherokees tell so many tales about them."

Farrell, who had been listening to all this in disapproving silence, said, "I think Grandfather was stupid to believe that stuff."

Jordan looked over at the boy for a long moment. Finally, he said, "Down deep, I'm not sure Asudi did believe in his stories as realities. I think rather that he wanted to believe."

Farrell sat up impatiently, brushing grass from his arms. "That's even crazier, if you ask me."

"No," Tiana said. "Jordan's right. Those stories came from the glorious Cherokee past. Maybe to Grandfather denying the stories would have been denying that past."

After a brief silence Jordan said, "I think that's one of the main differences between the younger members of the tribe and the Cherokees of Asudi's generation. The young people don't want to believe."

Farrell got to his feet with a sound of disgruntlement. "I'm hungry, sis. When can we eat?"

"Right now," Tiana agreed, feeling sad that Farrell did not seem to want to understand Asudi. She went to spread the picnic lunch on the ground.

They ate without much conversation, sitting on the grass, the food spread before them on the checkered tablecloth. Jordan complimented Tiana on her cooking, which pleased her. Inordinately, so it seemed to her, for, after all, she had been cooking for Farrell and Asudi for years. Only a dullard could fail to be fairly competent at it by now.

After they had eaten, they packed what remained of the food back into the picnic basket. Spreading the tablecloth and towels on the ground, Tiana and Jordan relaxed in the filtering shade of the elm tree while Farrell and Duke took a walk through the woods.

Tiana combed the tangles from her still-damp hair, then lay on her back, enjoying the feel of the warm rays of sunlight that made their way through the leaves overhead. Jordan stretched full-length on his side, facing Tiana, his head supported by one hand.

The afternoon was typical of June in Oklahoma—warm, still, somnolent with the drowsy keening of crickets. Later—in July and August—it would become hot and dry, the blazing stillness enervating. But June days were still verdant, with occasional showers to relieve the stultifying heat. Tiana was drifting into sleep when Jordan spoke beside her, the sound bringing her back to alertness.

"I'm glad you decided to come here with Farrell. He doesn't feel so alone as he might have otherwise. He's taken a great liking for Duke too. I'm beginning to think this arrangement might work out."

She turned her head and saw something in his eyes that put her on guard. The probing force of his gaze as it traveled up her slender body and settled on her face sent a tremor through her, setting a-tingle a confused jumble of emotions with which she was not equipped to deal. She felt her breasts tighten against the confining tautness of her maillot as she realized that his fingers were idly stroking the long silken strands of her hair that fanned out between them.

Her hand came up, ostensibly to smooth her hair, but she pushed his fingers determinedly away as she answered: "I hope you're right about things working out, Jordan. Farrell needs a man's influence in his life right now."

Avoiding his gaze, she sat up and reached for her cotton

43

shirt that lay on the grass nearby. From the corner of her eye, as she put the shirt on, she glimpsed the dawning cynicism in Jordan's gaze and the mocking curve of his mouth, and guessed he had intended to disarm her by talking of Farrell while his eyes and hands spoke another language altogether.

"What about you, Tiana?" he drawled lazily. "Don't you need anyone?"

Fastening the last button at the neck of the shirt, she viewed him with wary speculation. "I have Farrell and—if I should feel the need of anyone else, there's Dale—"

"I see." His lips thinned. "Are you sure that's enough?"

She thought they had settled this last night, but it seemed that Jordan did not give up so easily. He wasn't accustomed to being rebuffed by women. "Yes." Her chin jutted defensively. "I like my life, Jordan. It's comfortable and calm and satisfying." She paused. "I don't want the sort of emotional upheavals that some people seem to thrive on. Once, I—" She halted suddenly, aware that she had almost revealed more about her past life than she wished Jordan—or anyone—to know.

Jordan sat up slowly, his features taking on a hard expression. "It all sounds very dull to me," he muttered gruffly.

"I realize that," she said steadily, stooping to retrieve her jeans and stepping into them. "But it's *my* choice. We don't see things alike, and the sooner we both understand that, the better."

There was silence for a moment after that while they shook out the towels and tablecloth and folded them into the picnic basket.

"You've got a wall around you, Tiana," Jordan charged finally. "You're afraid to come out from behind it and find out what real life is all about."

"I don't see it that way." Her long silky lashes swept upward, and the smoldering mockery of his gaze was more bothersome than she was willing to admit. "Oh, Jordan," she said sadly. "Can't we just be friends?"

Suddenly she was aware of the tautness of his body, of his moist male smell that was somehow so unsettling. She could almost feel the hard muscles of his legs so near her own and longed, with an incomprehensible yearning, for something she did not understand.

"Of course," he said, but his voice was low and angry. "You don't want anybody getting too close. I'll go along with that." He turned away to fumble for his jeans and put them on. "Actually, you're something of a revelation, Tiana. I didn't think there were any Victorian women left in the world. That's funny, when you think about it—a Cherokee woman who has been totally westernized. A shame it couldn't have been a more modern concept that you chose to embrace."

Anger flared in her. First he had called her a spinster schoolmarm, and now a Victorian! It was almost as if he was trying to punish her for rebuffing him. "I—I suppose it makes you feel better to insult me!" she burst out jerkily, her hands going to snatch up the picnic basket and hold it against herself as if for protection, while he eyed her coldly.

"Not a whole lot," he replied, and then, as if his patience had spent itself, he walked past her and disappeared into the woods.

She gave him several minutes' head start before she followed, calling to Farrell that she was leaving. To her relief, Jordan was not in sight when she entered the house. She went directly to her bedroom where she showered, dressed in a sleeveless cotton dress and low-heeled sandals, and put her hair up. Then she want to the kitchen and started dinner preparations. Although Jordan was used to getting his own meals on the weekends, Tiana felt this was one task she could take over during her stay to free herself of any feeling of obligation to him.

Farrell came in and sat at the kitchen table, sunk again in his depressing gloom. Tiana let him be, feeling in no mood to try cheering him up. Later, when it was time to serve the casserole and salad she had prepared, she sent

45

Farrell to knock on the door of Jordan's studio and tell him dinner was ready.

Jordan's mood at dinner was amiable enough. Whatever perturbation he had felt toward Tiana seemed to have evaporated. Tiana put this down to the fact that she had, at last, made him understand her attitude toward the situation in which they found themselves. Perhaps they could be friends after all. As the meal progressed, she found herself relaxing. Even though Farrell refused to contribute anything to the conversation, Tiana was able to chat with Jordan about his painting and the planned exhibition in Paris in the fall.

After dinner Jordan said, "How about a game of back-gammon, Farrell?"

Farrell pushed back his hair and there was no interest in his dark eyes. "I don't know how to play," he muttered.

"It's not difficult. I'll teach you."

Farrell shook his head, his long hair swinging over his eyes. "Some other time. I'm not in the mood right now." Then he walked out of the room, leaving Tiana to try to smooth things over.

"Give him a little more time, Jordan."

His glance was doubtful. "I'm beginning to think he needs a good swift kick in the pants, rather than more time. Well, I'll try again with him tomorrow. How about you? Care to take me on in a game?"

"All right," she agreed readily. It would help them to feel more comfortable with each other, she decided. She was unwilling to admit how reluctant she was to part from him after the ease with which they had conversed over dinner. "Let me put the dishes in the dishwasher."

"I'll set up the board in the living room."

Hurriedly, Tiana cleared the table and carried the things into the kitchen. She was closing the dishwasher, after arranging the dishes inside, when she heard the doorbell ring. She entered the living room just as Jordan was opening the door.

"Hi, honey! Mohammed won't come to the mountain so

46

the mountain . . ." The blond woman who had stepped into the room carried a brown paper bag and her voice trailed off as she saw Tiana standing near the kitchen doorway. Her blue eyes flew to Jordan's face and her smile went from being mischievous to being forced. "Mercy, honey, I didn't know you had company. Or is this your housekeeper?" It was clear to Tiana that the woman, whoever she was, meant the question as a dig.

Farrell had drifted back into the living room at the sound of the bell and came to a stop beside Tiana. The blonde was wearing a blue crepe halter-topped pantsuit that left little of her figure to the imagination. She took another step toward Jordan and laid a familiar hand on his arm. "This must be your little ward, Jordan. Aren't you going to introduce me?"

Jordan flashed the blonde a wry smile. "Lois, this is Farrell Vann—and his sister, Tiana. Farrell, Tiana, meet Lois Graham."

Lois Graham. The name rang a vague bell in Tiana's mind. The woman owned a business in Tahlequah—a dress shop, wasn't it? Yes, now that she thought about it, she had heard Jordan's name linked with Lois Graham's. Incredibly, this overblown sexpot must be his current flame. Then, abruptly, Tiana remembered hearing Jordan's parting words to Millie when the housekeeper left Friday evening. He'd asked her to call Lois and break their date for tonight. Clearly, Lois hadn't wanted to accept that.

"Hi, Farrell," Lois was saying brightly. "Oh, honey, he's cute. You're a lucky boy, you know, having Jordan for a guardian." Her mascaraed lashes lifted as her gaze swept over Jordan possessively. Then she looked at Tiana. "And you're Farrell's sister? How convenient that you could come for a visit. I understand Jordan is an old friend of your family's."

"Yes," said Tiana tightly, feeling her hackles rising. Everything about this woman irritated her. *Heavens, how could Jordan stand all that gushing and eyelash fluttering?* But then, Tiana told herself cynically, Jordan's thoughts seemed to be on Lois Graham's other "charms." The way he was looking at her now made Tiana positively nauseated.

Lois had turned all her attention on Jordan now. "Honey, I brought the steaks. I thought I'd fix a nice little dinner and—"

Jordan stood looking down at Lois with his hands in his trouser pockets, a maddeningly imperturbable grin on his face. "We've already eaten, I'm afraid, Lois. If you'd let me know—"

"Oh, that's all right." Lois brushed this aside with one fluttering sweep of a well-manicured hand. "We can still have the wine." She glanced coyly over her shoulder at Tiana. "Maybe your friend and her brother would like to join us."

"I've got other things to do," said Farrell, his face an expressionless mask. "I'm going to my room." He left Tiana's side and ran down the stairs to the lower level.

"Why don't you get us some glasses, Tiana?" Jordan inquired. There was a challenge in his measuring glance.

Bristling, Tiana turned on her heel and walked back into the kitchen. She got two wine glasses from the cabinet, carried them into the living room, and set them down on the coffee table. By that time Jordan was sprawled on the leather couch with the simpering Lois curled up at his side. If she were any closer, Tiana thought mutinously, she'd be on top of him!

"Here are your glasses," Tiana said shortly. "I'm sure you two will excuse me." She turned away, but not before she had caught a glimpse of Jordan's lopsided grin.

"This is much cozier, anyway," she heard Lois purring as she left the room. "Isn't it, hon? Just the two of us—"

How disgusting! Tiana sneered to herself as she shut her bedroom door behind her. She paced across the room, fuming. Odd, but she had actually been looking forward to playing backgammon with Jordan. She had thought *he* was looking forward to it, too. But any idea of a tame backgammon game had certainly flown out of his head when the voluptuous Lois appeared. He hadn't even mentioned it again! It was sickening how a woman like that could get her way with men!

Tiana stopped in her pacing, amazed at herself. Why was she so angry? Why should she care if Jordan entertained fifteen sexy women in his living room? Why should she care if he had a veritable orgy! It was no concern of hers.

Determinedly, she changed into a nightgown, brushed out her hair, and climbed into bed with a book. Occasionally, the sound of Lois Graham's high-pitched laugh reached her through the closed bedroom door, but she pushed away any questions as to what Jordan and his blonde were doing in the living room. After discovering that she had read the same paragraph three times and still did not know what it said, she put the book aside and switched off the light. She lay there a long time before she fell asleep.

Sunday morning Tiana, dressed in white slacks and a yellow knit shirt, set scrambled eggs, bacon, and toast on the dining room table. Farrell seemed to be in slightly better spirits; he actually made a few comments without being prodded. Tiana could have done without his enthusiastic, "That Lois Graham is some looker, isn't she?"

As for Jordan, he appeared at breakfast wearing paint-streaked jeans and a white T-shirt and looking a little tired around the eyes.

As he took his seat, he addressed Farrell. "I'll be working in the studio this morning, but I thought we might give the horses some exercise this afternoon. How does that sound to you?"

To Tiana's surprise, Farrell said, "Okay. What time?"

"About one," Jordan said and Farrell nodded and turned his attention to ladling strawberry jam onto his toast.

"Care to join us, Tiana?" Jordan asked casually.

"No, thank you." She was determined to keep her distance from Jordan after his disgusting display with Lois

Graham the night before. She wondered when Lois had gone home. Tiana herself had lain awake very late, and the woman was still there when she fell asleep. No wonder Jordan looked tired, she thought bitterly.

Jordan appeared completely unruffled by her refusal to join in the horseback ride. Apparently he didn't feel he needed her as an intermediary with Farrell anymore. He must think he was winning Farrell over and, indeed, her brother did seem less belligerent than the night before. He had even agreed to the ride alone with Jordan. No doubt he had been impressed with Jordan's savoir-faire in handling a female of Lois Graham's type. Of course Tiana wanted the two of them to be friends. Only now that she suspected it was about to happen, she felt oddly unnecessary.

Don't be silly, she scolded herself silently. It would be nice to have the house to herself that afternoon. She could do some laundry and get ready for her first day of classes on Monday.

Perversely, when it came time for Jordan and Farrell to leave for their ride, Tiana half-wished Jordan would ask her again to accompany them. She followed them to the front door, saying, "Enjoy yourself, Farrell, but don't try any of your daring rodeo tricks until the horse gets to know you."

Farrell grimaced. "You don't need to give me instructions, sis. I've been riding since I could walk."

She smiled fondly at him. "I know, but sometimes you take unnecessary chances." She glanced at Jordan, who was listening to this exchange with seeming impatience to be off. "You will keep an eye on him, won't you?"

His expression was not encouraging, and his "He's a big boy now, Tiana" was not what she had hoped to hear. Cheeks burning, she walked quickly back into the house.

Jordan and Farrell returned at dusk. After washing up, they sat down immediately to the cold ham salad and fruit compote Tiana had prepared in their absence.

"I got to ride an Arabian named Omar," Farrell told Tiana, his eyes alight. "He's a beauty. Jordan says I can ride him any time I want."

"That's fine," she replied, thinking that Jordan was very clever at breaking down her brother's defenses. First the collie, then Lois, and now a horse.

But Farrell's cheerful mood was dashed by Jordan's next words. "Do you have any leads on a job, Farrell?"

The boy glanced at him quickly and then looked at his plate. "No—not exactly. I mean, I guess I'll go into town and look around one day soon."

"Maybe that won't be necessary," Jordan said. "I need someone to work around here."

"Doing what?" Farrell asked suspiciously.

"Taking care of the yard and the horses, fencing a pasture, painting the trim on the house—things like that. I'm sure I could keep you busy all summer, and I'll pay the going rate. You'd save money by not having to pay for transportation into town."

"Well, I don't know—" Farrell hesitated. He did not seem to be overjoyed by the offer. Tiana suspected, not for the first time, that he really had no desire to work at all. This was a trait in her brother that deeply concerned her, yet she did think that Jordan might have chosen a more propitious time to spring the news on him.

"I'm sure when you think about it you'll agree you probably can't do better in town," Jordan continued, ignoring Farrell's lack of enthusiasm. "You can start in the morning. I'll outline some chores for you at breakfast. Let's say eight to five, with an hour off for lunch."

Farrell was silent while he digested this information, his face working, as if he were having an inner struggle. Then he placed his napkin beside his plate and said, "I'm going to take Duke for a walk."

When he was gone, Tiana finished her dinner quickly and carried her dishes into the kitchen. Jordan, who had been lingering over his second cup of coffee, appeared in

51

the kitchen doorway, leaning one shoulder against the frame.

"I get the feeling you don't approve of my plans for Farrell."

Tiana switched off the faucet and turned from the sink, wiping her hands on a towel which lay on the cabinet top. His eyes surveyed her intently.

"I didn't think you needed my approval."

He half-smiled. "It's not that I need it, but I'm curious as to why you're not more supportive of my decision. You're the one who said Farrell has too much time on his hands."

"It's kind of you to offer Farrell a job," she said, leaning back against the cabinet and linking her fingers together. "But your timing could hardly have been worse. Just when he was starting to loosen up with you . . ."

He straightened, thrusting his hands into his jeans' pockets. "I fail to see what would be gained by allowing Farrell to mope around here for another week or two with nothing to do. It seems to me that idleness was behind his irresponsible behavior in the past."

"Since you seem to have everything figured out, why talk to me about it?" Tiana retorted stiffly.

He continued to eye her thoughtfully. "You're awfully touchy today. Didn't you sleep well last night? I hope Lois and I didn't disturb you."

"Not in the way you seem to think," she flared. "I didn't find that inane giggling that went on half the night particularly restful. However, since this is your house, I am hardly in a position to complain."

"If I didn't know better, I'd have a sneaking suspicion that you're a wee bit jealous."

Tiana did not reply. Jordan lifted himself onto the balls of his feet for a moment and studied her deliberately. Tiana turned away, busying her hands with stacking dishes into the dishwasher. He was just trying to infuriate her, and he was not going to get away with it.

"Tiana?"

She sighed and turned. "What do you want?"

"Aren't you going to deny that you're jealous?"

"I don't intend to dignify such blatant egotism with a denial," she countered, with an attempt at a coolness she did not feel.

He did not answer, but merely moved farther into the room, looking tall and lean and somehow threatening. Tiana's hand went up to smooth her chignon, and she turned away, deliberately picking up the dish cloth and swiping at the cabinet top.

"You let me know at the lake yesterday that your interest in me is solely as Farrell's guardian. You wouldn't be regretting that decision now, would you?"

He was standing very close to her, and she turned completely around to look up at him, feeling the sharp edge of the countertop against her backbone. She pressed her lips together, seeing the dangerous glint in Jordan's dark eyes, and summoned her skittering thoughts to protect herself. "Good Lord, does your conceit know no bounds? Do you think every woman you meet has a—a personal interest in you? What a featherbrained bunch of ninnies you must think us!"

"My opinion of women is not totally favorable, I admit. My experience with them has convinced me that they are not a particularly trustworthy lot."

His face seemed to harden as he spoke these words, and Tiana wondered what had caused his cynical outlook. At the same time, she couldn't help being insulted by his assessment of all females. "You are not above using them for your own ends, though, are you, Jordan? I didn't notice any reluctance on your part last night when Lois Graham was coming on like a—piranha!"

"Ah-ha! Lois again. Well, what was I supposed to do? I merely enjoyed an evening with a woman who appreciated my company. Is that a crime?"

"Apparently not in your code of ethics," Tiana said, the words dripping with sarcasm. "I didn't think it possible, but I am actually beginning to feel sorry for that woman!"

He caught her angrily by the shoulders, shaking her. "Don't waste your sympathy on Lois! She's not a bundle of hang-ups and frustrations. If you want to feel sorry for someone, Tiana, look to yourself."

Tiana was aghast. "How dare you! The nerve—"

"Oh, yes, Tiana, you will find that I have enough nerve for both of us!"

His hands, which still rested on her shoulders, moved down her back, his arms pulling her relentlessly against him. Tiana struggled desperately, feeling a rising panic, but she only succeeded in moving her body against the muscular length of his, which caused a violent increase in her pulse rate. She could hear her own breath coming swiftly as, suddenly, there did not seem to be enough air to draw into her lungs. She could feel the heat of his body, the iron muscles of his chest crushed against her breasts, and smell the faint odor of shaving lotion.

Staring up at him, her eyes wide, she realized that his mouth, only inches from her own, was twisted mockingly, his eyes glinting with triumph. "Stop fighting, Tiana. Haven't you learned by now that there are more effective ways to bend a man to your will?"

Tiana heard her heart pounding and abruptly she sensed a change in him. One moment he was holding her cruelly, deriding her efforts to free herself, and the next she saw strange lights moving in the depths of his eyes. He stared at her for a long moment, while a frown flitted across his face and was gone. Then, with a muffled exclamation, he bent his head and covered her lips, his mouth moving slowly, parting her own. There was such practiced ease in the languid, sensuous way he was kissing her that she felt all her senses rousing to full awareness and her resistance slipping away. She no longer had the strength or the desire to struggle; instead, she had a shocking impulse to wind her arms around his neck and pull him even closer.

As the seconds passed, she seemed to forget everything— where she was, her antagonism toward this man, and the insults he had heaped upon her—everything except the feel of his body and his warm, demanding lips. But then, when it was almost too late, she seemed to move outside herself, to view what was happening, and to feel humiliated and furious with herself. With a vast effort of will, she shoved at him with her hands against his chest, turning her face aside.

Taken unaware, Jordan stepped back, his arms falling away. He stared at her with smoldering eyes that grew cold as she watched. "So . . ." he said, sucking in a harsh breath. "There is a small crack in that wall, after all."

Tiana buried her face in her hands. "Leave me alone," she muttered unsteadily.

Jordan stiffened. "Still feel sorry for Lois?"

"Get away from me!" Tiana clenched her fists. "For heaven's sake, stop being so darned smug! Leave me alone and let me think. I—I can't stay here now. I—" Her head was throbbing and she felt as weak as a kitten.

"Quit flaunting your stupid pride in my face," Jordan exploded. "Asudi's cabin has already been rented and you can't afford to stay anywhere else. My God, must you make a federal case out of a simple kiss?"

A simple kiss. For him, maybe, but far from simple for her. Never had she responded to a man with such stunning sensations of dark passion. She was shocked and revolted—and confused. Tiana sank wearily into one of the kitchen chairs. "Please," she said weakly. "Go away."

Jordan smiled sardonically and walked toward the door. "All right, Tiana," he said quietly. "But stop looking so tragic. You just joined the human race, that's all."

4

Tiana was beginning to think Dale had forgotten their lunch date when she saw him threading his way through the crowded little restaurant near the university campus. Dale Gregory had Indian blood, as did a majority of the people who lived in and around Tahlequah, the capital of the old Cherokee nation, where some places of business announced themselves on the facades of their buildings in both English and Cherokee. Dale was, in fact, one-eighth Cherokee and one-eighth Creek, but the Indian ancestry was hardly discernible. He was thirty years old, medium tall and blockily built, with hazel eyes and sand-colored hair. His features were pleasant rather than handsome, but Tiana had been attracted by his calm, unruffled manner and the feeling he gave her that he would never ask more of her than she was willing to give. Once she had suspected that he was about to broach the subject of marriage, but she had quickly diverted the conversation and he, picking up on the ploy, had not veered toward such personal areas again. Tiana had been sufficiently uncertain of her own feelings to accept with equanimity the unhurried pace of their courtship.

At the moment there was a small frown between his sandy brows, but his face cleared when he caught sight of her, and he smiled.

"Am I late? Tiana, I'm sorry. . . ." He pulled out a chair and sat down facing her. "You look beautiful. Is that a new dress?" He gave her time only for a negative shake of the head before he went on. "Harris and I got involved in the teaching schedules for next term and I lost all track of time." Harris was Tahlequah's elementary school guidance counselor. "Am I forgiven?"

"Of course." Dale talked frequently of his job and the school activities with which they were both involved. He liked his work in spite of frequent complaints about the poor state of educators' salaries, and Tiana enjoyed his tales of intrigue in the administrative offices. Dale was outgoing, affectionate in an undemanding sort of way, and seemed to her to be perfect husband material, in case she should ever decide she wanted a husband.

They perused their menus. The restaurant was one of their frequent eating places, and the waitress smiled and joked with Dale as she took their order for baked trout and coffee. As the waitress moved away, Dale asked, "How did your first class go?"

"Very well," she said. "There's going to be quite a bit of outside work, but I think I'll get some new ideas for classroom use. I've heard the class that meets this afternoon is pretty tough, though."

"I hope there won't be *too* much work out of class. I had hoped we'd see a lot of each other this summer. I was disappointed when you broke our date the other night. I know you said you were tired, but—"

Tiana felt her muscles tightening as she broke in quickly, "Dale . . ." She paused, biting her lower lip. "I couldn't explain things over the phone Saturday. I've had a rather chaotic weekend." She saw him frown and added, "You remember I told you that Farrell and I had an appointment with Grandfather's attorney Thursday?"

"Sure, I remember."

"Well, things did not go exactly as I had hoped." She hesitated again, and then decided that she might as well tell him everything—or almost everything—and have done with it. He would hear it by the grapevine very soon, anyway. "Grandfather named Jordan Ridge as Farrell's guardian until he's eighteen. Jordan insisted that Farrell move in with him, and he said that I might as well come for the summer, too. At first I thought it was a preposterous idea, but then I realized it was the only way I could be with Farrell. Anyway, Farrell and I moved to Jordan Ridge's house Friday afternoon. Then Jordan thought we should all stay at home over the weekend so that Farrell would start feeling more comfortable there."

As she was speaking, Dale's brows drew together. He fiddled with his fork, regarding her silently. Then he said slowly, "Jordan Ridge—isn't that the painter?"

Something in his voice made her feel defensive. She looked at him anxiously. "Yes, and I know what people say about artists, but he spends most of his time in his studio. And he's given Farrell a job."

"Never mind *artists*, Tiana. It wouldn't matter if Jordan Ridge was a carpenter—or a ditch digger. I don't think your living in his house is a very good idea."

"I did try to talk him out of taking Farrell. I said we could manage very well in the cabin, but he wouldn't listen. He did have a point, Dale. You know how unruly Farrell has been lately. Jordan seems to know how to handle him—better than I can, anyway."

Dale's expression did not reflect understanding. Instead his hazel eyes fastened on her face with concern in them. Carefully, he said, "I know Jordan Ridge is a great painter—the best. I admire his work. But frankly, Tiana, his reputation in other areas is not quite so sterling. He's had relationships with some pretty—well, loose women."

She felt the blood warming her face and her dark eyes widened. "You don't think that I would . . ." Her voice broke off confusedly and she swallowed. "Dale, surely you don't imagine I'd become involved with a man like that!"

He leaned across the table, taking her hand. "It isn't that I distrust you, Tiana. There's never been a hint of a shadow on your reputation," he said gently, but his face reflected uncertainty. "To be honest, though, I'm not sure even *your* reputation can withstand four months living under the same roof with Jordan Ridge."

Tiana was surprised by this strongly negative reaction

from Dale, who had always been the most reasonable of men. Never, by word or action, had he given her any indication that he had a jealous bone in his body. Yet she couldn't help suspecting that jealousy was behind his objections, rather than any concern for her reputation. The waitress appeared before she could reply, placing a steaming platter of trout and baked potato in front of her. When she was gone, Tiana said, "I don't think people are shocked by things like that anymore. I think the real reason you don't want me living there is that you're not all that sure of my resistance to someone like Jordan."

He shrugged. "That's not fair, Tiana. I know you're not sleeping with the man."

"Sleeping with him?" Her voice rose shrilly and, to her deep embarrassment, drew the glances of the men at the next table.

Dale's face flushed. "I'm sorry. I shouldn't have said that. I've never for a moment suspected you of playing around behind my back."

"Then why did you say it?" she asked stiffly.

"I was just trying to make my point," he said a little uneasily. "I put it badly, I know." He gave her a rueful smile. "Honey, you know that anyone connected with the public school system in a town this size has to be concerned about his image. You can't flaunt community standards without paying the consequences." He broke off, obviously uncertain as to how to phrase what he wanted to say. "We both have to be concerned about that, whether we like it or not. Some day we may want to—uh, make a commitment to each other, and I wouldn't want something like that hanging over our heads."

"I think I'm beginning to get the point," she said curtly. "You're worried about what this might do to *your* reputation, aren't you, Dale? You're afraid someone might think you're being—what is that old-fashioned term?—cuckolded."

"No," he protested. "It's just that I know there will be speculation around town when this gets out."

"I don't see why that should concern us, as long as *we* know there's no truth to any rumors of that kind."

"Well, yes, but—" He stammered, thrown by her logic. "Tiana, you don't have any experience handling a man like Ridge. Okay, okay—I'll shut up, but think about what I've said."

They finished their lunch in silence. Tiana ate only half of her fish before she pushed the plate away, her mind filled with conflicting thoughts. "Dale, would you object if someone like George McNair had been appointed Farrell's guardian and I'd moved into *his* house?"

"No, of course not, but he's not a notorious womanizer."

She gripped her hands together in her lap. After a moment, she said, "I'll tell you again that I have no interest in any kind of a relationship with Jordan Ridge. If you can't accept my word for that, then it seems to me you don't trust me at all."

"I've said I trust you. . . ." he began, his voice trailing away under her steady gaze.

"Then don't suggest again that I move away and leave Farrell."

Dale sighed deeply. "People will . . ." He fell silent.

"People," Tiana said ironically.

"Tiana, I have strong protective feelings for you," he said appealingly, leaning toward her, his voice low.

Her expression was guarded for a second, as she looked at him, then the tenseness drained out of her and her dark eyes smiled at him. The sincerity in his appeal warmed her.

They ate dessert with a much more comfortable atmosphere at the table, engaging in a discussion about some new remedial reading kits that Dale had ordered for the elementary school. Tiana felt grateful to him for talking of impersonal things. By the time they left the restaurant she was feeling a warm glow of affection for him. On the sidewalk he put an arm around her shoulders and walked her back to the university where, behind a sheltering semicircle of shrubbery, he kissed her briefly and gently, a kiss that was in no way akin to the brute force with which Jordan

61

had kissed her the day before. In her mind she compared the two, telling herself she preferred Dale's undemanding warmth.

"Let's meet for lunch Wednesday," he suggested, smiling down at her. "Maybe we can make some plans for the weekend."

"Fine," she murmured, touching his face tentatively with the tips of her fingers before parting from him to enter the brick classroom building.

Tiana's closest friend and fellow teacher at her elementary school was a tall, willowy redhead named Nancy Pearson. Nancy was enrolled in Tiana's afternoon class and, since they both arrived outside the classroom a few minutes early, they were able to get seats together near the back. Tiana had known Nancy for two years; the two young women had begun their teaching careers in adjacent classrooms. Nancy Pearson had proved far less intense about her teaching duties than Tiana, who, on the rebound from her broken engagement, had embraced the job as if it were a lifeline thrown to her in deep water just before she went down for the third time. Still, Nancy was not incompetent, even if she approached her job with the casual good humor of a girl whose nature it was not take anything *too* seriously. She had frequently urged Tiana to move into Tahlequah and share her four-room apartment, promising to "fix up" Tiana with one or two of the small town's most dashing bachelors. Nancy had a number of male friends, but no permanent relationship in her life, and this seemed to suit her well. Unwilling to leave Farrell and Asudi, Tiana had always refused the invitations to share her friend's living quarters. Now that she would be forced to move to town in the fall when she left Jordan's, the idea seemed more attractive than it ever had in the past—particularly if Farrell decided to go out on his own when he reached his majority—and she decided to talk to Nancy about it when there was more time.

"I had lunch in the university cafeteria," Nancy said,

grinning, when the two were settled into adjacent chairs. "I thought I might run into you there."

"I had lunch with Dale," Tiana told her. "Let's have lunch Wednesday—oops, no, I promised Dale. How about Friday?"

"Okay." Nancy made a face. "Still seeing our up-and-coming principal regularly, are you?" For reasons which Tiana had never entirely understood, Nancy did not like Dale very well. Since he was her superior on the job, she managed to be friendly enough to him but she had, on several occasions, made disparaging remarks about him to Tiana, usually to the effect that he was a cool customer or a bootpolisher.

"Yes, I am," Tiana said.

Nancy studied Tiana with her clear green eyes for a moment. "So help me, I can't see Dale Gregory as a romantic figure. What do you talk about—school?"

"Among other things," Tiana replied, bridling a little at Nancy's flippant tone.

"Well, I know I'm probably biased, but I just can't see him getting passionate—or excited about anything, except maybe climbing the job ladder."

Tiana fingered the textbook and spiral notebook which lay on her desk. "You should have seen him a little while ago. He got pretty excited when I told him where I'm living for the summer!"

Nancy looked at her blankly. "Where *are* you living?"

Momentarily, Tiana had forgotten that Nancy knew nothing of the things that had transpired during the last few days. Briefly, she told her of the provisions of Asudi's will and the move to Jordan Ridge's house.

Nancy's eyes narrowed. "So Dale disapproves? Oh, wait a minute—Jordan Ridge. He's that painter—that gorgeous hunk of man. No wonder Dale objected!"

Tiana opened her spiral notebook and began to doodle idly in the margin, her face tight. Again she felt warmth creeping up her cheeks. Nancy's description of Jordan had recalled the way he had kissed her with vivid detail, and anger and shame made her bite her lip.

"Hey, kiddo, all of a sudden you've got this secretive look on your face," Nancy said bluntly. "Don't tell me something actually happened out there at Ridge's place over the weekend."

Tiana drew a precise square on the page in front of her. "Happened?" she fenced, seemingly engrossed in making a neat four-sided box.

"Tiana, you never looked that way when Dale's name was mentioned," Nancy said, her voice speculative.

"What way?" Tiana gazed at her, puzzled.

Nancy shrugged, "I don't know—embarrassed, sort of—or helpless."

"Oh, fiddle," Tiana said dismissingly.

Nancy folded back the cover of her notepad and positioned it in the center of her desk, a ballpoint pen beside it. "The two of you did spend the weekend in the country together, though."

"What a way of putting it!" Tiana protested. "Jordan and I aren't alone in the house, you know. Farrell is there—and the housekeeper, too, on weekdays. Besides, Jordan spends a great deal of time in his studio. He's totally absorbed in his work. We did have a picnic and go for a swim Saturday, but that was only so that the three of us could get better acquainted."

"A picnic and swim!" Nancy's gaze was avidly curious. "What did Dale have to say about that?"

Tiana sighed. "I didn't exactly go into detail about my weekend activities. He was already a little hurt because I'd cancelled our date for Saturday night to stay out there with Farrell. Of course, I know he would understand."

Nancy faked a coughing sound.

"Does that mean you think Dale *wouldn't* understand?"

"It doesn't mean anything," Nancy said. "I've no idea what Dale thinks. After all, I don't know him as well as you do."

"That's right," Tiana said testily, "you don't." She

glanced at the wall clock and saw that it was only two minutes until time for the class to start. Most of the seats were filled already.

Then she looked back at Nancy, sighing. "I'm sorry. I didn't mean to cut you off like that."

Nancy's smile was ungrudging. "It's okay. I'm too outspoken. I'm sure you have your reasons for wanting to live out there for the summer. I can't help worrying about you a little, though. You're such a child when it comes to men. I just wonder if you would recognize danger if it fell on you."

Tiana laughed, genuinely amused. "What a switch! You've always told me I don't take enough chances. You're the try-anything-once girl."

Nancy frowned slightly, causing two fine lines to appear in her ordinarily smooth, pale forehead. "That's just my point. You're too rigid. Everything has to be planned down to the last detail. I don't mean to sound judgmental, but there has never seemed to me to be anything spontaneous in your relationship with Dale Gregory. It's as if you have your whole life arranged and can't see anything extraneous to the arrangement. I'm afraid that if you're ever forced to deal with something outside that rigid little outline, you might go over the edge."

Tiana stared at her. "What in heaven's name are you talking about?"

"Jordan Ridge," said Nancy, green eyes holding brown eyes unblinkingly.

A tightness invaded Tiana's chest. Her eyes faltered and fell away and she ran a slim hand over her cheek to hide her expression. "I—I wonder where the professor is."

"Changing the subject, eh?" Nancy asked, after a pause.

"You have always been too imaginative," Tiana said without meeting her friend's look. "And you exaggerate deplorably."

"Tiana, regardless of what I think of Dale, he's got good reason to object to your present living arrangement. I've heard stories about how Jordan Ridge operates. I can't believe he'll overlook a young, attractive female living in his own house. It's the perfect set-up for—"

"Oh, stop it!" Tiana said angrily. "Jordan tries his line on every halfway presentable woman he meets. I'm sure he's lost count of his conquests. Why, he spent Saturday evening in his living room with a—a blonde bombshell."

"Uh-huh . . ." Nancy murmured. "I thought you said he's totally absorbed in his work. Doesn't sound like it to me."

"Do you really think I'm foolish enough to allow myself to become just another woman in a long, long list?" The depth of the bitterness that edged her words surprised even herself.

Nancy gazed at her with an expression of dawning understanding. "So you're going to be the exception?" she asked. "You're going to prove to the world—and to yourself—that you can live for months under the same roof with him without falling under his spell?"

Momentarily, Tiana looked surprised. Then she shrugged with weary acquiescence. "That's not exactly the way I would put it, but yes—if you care to see it like that."

Nancy shook her head, causing soft red waves to bounce about her face. "Lots of luck, kiddo." She looked toward the classroom door and lowered her voice. "Here comes the professor." Her glance flew to the wall clock. "Nine minutes after. Amazing timing. Another minute and we could have all walked out with no absence against our names."

"What do you mean?" Tiana whispered huskily.

Nancy's green eyes looked at her with total innocence. "The handbook says students are required to wait only ten minutes after the appointed time for a class."

"Not that!" Tiana whispered. "What did you mean by wishing me luck in that doubtful tone of voice?"

Nancy glanced furtively at the professor, who was now leaning on the podium and taking a rubber band from around a stack of student cards in preparation for calling the roll. She bent closer and said in a low voice, "You're setting yourself up for trouble, Tiana. I don't care how much you deny it, your reaction earlier tells me you are not unaware of Jordan Ridge's attractions. If you are as transparent to *him* as you are to me, heaven help you. And Dale isn't stupid, either. He's not going to stand by and—"

"Dale trusts me," Tiana protested. "We trust each other. It's the only kind of relationship worth having. And I'm *not* attracted to Jordan."

"Maybe not, and maybe you just won't admit it to yourself," Nancy conceded, "but you're not in love with Dale, either. If you were, you'd have progressed beyond the chaste kisses I've seen the two of you exchange. Know what I think? I think you chose Dale for that very reason. You feel safe with him. No emotional entanglements or disturbing impulses. Wow, some guy must have hurt you badly the way you defend yourself."

The assessment stunned Tiana. She looked toward the front of the class as the professor began roll call. The room had grown quiet. She picked up her pen and scribbled on her notebook: "You don't know how I feel about Dale!" She pushed the note toward Nancy, who read, then scribbled a reply.

"Oh, yeah? What do you feel when Dale kisses you?"

Tiana felt an uncomfortable warmth as she read the tart question and she did not answer—in writing or in any other way. But as the long roll call progressed, the disturbing question would not leave her mind. During the two years she had known Nancy Pearson, she had learned that the flighty redhead was, oddly, a shrewd judge of people. Nancy was flippant, impulsive, and disorganized, but she was also generous and intelligent and a very good friend. She probably knew Tiana as well as anyone in the world, and Tiana found it difficult to ignore her probing question. What *did* she feel when Dale kissed her? Certainly not sky-rockets or flashing lights! But could a lasting relationship be based on anything so fleeting as sexual excitement? She wanted no part of the torrid, usually brief affairs which

Jordan indulged in—if the rumors could be believed. The very idea made her feel physically sick.

Trust. That was of foremost importance to her, and she had that with Dale. They were always honest with each other. She admitted, for the first time, that her failure to tell Dale of the picnic and swim with Jordan, not to mention that crazy moment in the kitchen, was pricking her conscience. She had never kept anything like that from him before. But if she should describe to Dale that shocking kiss . . .

Her fingers twisted the pen nervously on the desk in front of her. If Dale knew that, would he believe that she hadn't welcomed it? What other things might he suspect her of as the summer progressed?

She couldn't tell Dale. She didn't want to lose his trust; the relationship was important to her. Maybe it wasn't the love affair of the century, but she admired everything about Dale. She felt secure with him, she enjoyed his company, and they had so much in common.

Despairingly, she said to herself, "It will grow into love in time." Somehow, though, the words which rang in her mind lacked conviction. Yet she had to believe that the kind of love that made a good marriage was composed of affection and mutual respect and admiration, not a shallow physical awareness, however strong.

Suddenly, she became aware that Nancy was nudging her arm. She looked up, startled.

"Is there a Miss Tiana Vann here, please?" The professor was glancing about the room as if he had called her name before.

"Yes—present," she said clearly, then sank back in her chair, overcome with a sudden desire to leave the classroom and be alone for a while.

Beside her, she noticed in one brief glimpse, Nancy was looking at her with sympathy.

The hour eventually came to an end and Tiana bid her friend a hasty good-bye, hurried to the parking lot, and drove out of town, her mood still subdued. When she reached the house, she found Millie Carver in the kitchen and gleaned the information that Jordan was still closeted in his studio. Gratefully, she accepted a glass of iced tea from Millie and retired to her room to start the reading assignments in preparation for her day of classes on Wednesday.

She found it hard to concentrate on reading but, determined, she plowed through three chapters for Wednesday morning's class and jotted down a few ideas to contribute to class discussion. She heard Farrell moving about in his room a little after five and went to ask about his first day of work. He had been painting the trim at the back of the house and his arms and shirt were generously splattered with brown.

Farrell had collapsed across his bed and he rolled his head to look up at Tiana. "How was it?" she asked wearily.

"Backbreaking—and boring. I thought five o'clock would never come!"

"Maybe if you had a radio to listen to, time would go faster," Tiana said encouragingly. "Would you like to borrow my portable tomorrow?"

Farrell closed his eyes and sighed deeply. "Can I use your car tonight?"

"Oh, Farrell, I don't know. You're so tired. Don't you think—"

He sat up, glowering at her. "Stop sounding like my mother! Can I use your car or can't I?"

"I really can't afford to give you gas money, and the tank is less than half full."

"I'll pay you back when I get my first paycheck."

"Where are you planning to go?"

"I can't give you a minute-by-minute schedule," Farrell retorted belligerently, "so get off my back! I'd like to see somebody besides you and Jordan and that Carver woman. Did you know she whistles while she works? I had to listen to that half the day. It just about drove me nuts."

Tiana suppressed a smile. "I'll think about the car and let you know later." She made for the door. "I'll see you at dinner. Millie says it'll be at seven, so you have time for a nap before getting cleaned up."

She retreated to her bedroom again, where she started the reading assignment for Wednesday afternoon's class. About six thirty she went out to the kitchen to help Millie finish the dinner preparations.

Jordan emerged from his bedroom just at seven, having bathed and changed into clean jeans and shirt after a day of painting that had started at dawn. He looked exhausted, and Tiana hoped that Farrell had better sense than to bring up the subject of going into town over dinner.

Farrell, however, did not. They had only begun eating when he asked Tiana, "How about the car, sis? You said you'd think about it."

Before Tiana could open her mouth, Jordan looked up and asked, "What's this? Do you have need of a car tonight, Farrell?"

Farrell, realizing his mistake too late, stammered an evasive reply which was cut off in mid-sentence. "Am I to understand that you have no plans, but merely wish to take your sister's car out for a joyride?"

"No," denied Farrell hotly. "I want to go into town and see a couple of my friends."

"Jordan—" Tiana tried to come to Farrell's rescue. "I don't mind—"

"Just a minute, Tiana," snapped Jordan, still looking at his ward. "What do you and your friends plan to do?"

Farrell squirmed in his seat. "Just mess around."

"You'll have to be more specific than that," said Jordan with heavy sarcasm.

Farrell glared at him with ill-concealed resentment. "We'll probably to to a drive-in movie or roller skating."

"Anything else?" pressed Jordan.

Farrell's glance went to Tiana. "*Can* I have the car?"

Jordan laid down his fork and penned Farrell with a penetrating look. "Let's get something understood, Farrell. Hereafter, when you make plans, you will clear them with me. I'm going to allow you to go into town this evening.

70

You may take my jeep. It has a full tank of gas, and I don't want it returned empty. Nor do I want to learn later that you've been speeding or engaging in any other risky activities. You will be back by ten thirty."

"Ten thirty!" Farrell looked at him with incredulity. "The movie doesn't even start until eight and it's a half-hour's drive out here."

"Perhaps you should go skating then," said Jordan levelly. "Now that you're doing tiring physical work every day, you need plenty of rest. If you need any money, I'll advance you ten dollars against your first paycheck."

Farrell stared at him for a moment and finally murmured a grudging assent.

Jordan handed him a ten-dollar bill and the keys to the jeep. They finished the meal in silence. Tiana fumed all the while. He was being too hard on Farrell! It was all she could do not to blurt this out in front of her brother. The only thing that stopped her was the knowledge that any attempt to undermine Jordan's authority would work to Farrell's detriment. He needed discipline, she admitted, but surely not the harsh variety that Jordan was imposing.

At length, Farrell excused himself and started for the door. Jordan's words stopped him halfway across the living room. "Don't be late. If for some reason you are unavoidably detained, call to let us know. Otherwise, if you're late, you will not be allowed to go anywhere for two weeks. Do we understand each other?"

Clearly furious, Farrell nodded curtly and left the house, shutting the door behind him as firmly as he dared.

A heavy silence followed Farrell's departure. Jordan glanced at Tiana with a set expression. "Go ahead and say it. You're going to explode if you don't."

"All right, I will!" Tiana put down her coffee cup and faced him squarely. "You're treating him like a—an inmate in a reform school!"

"You're entitled to your opinion," he drawled, "but it occurs to me that what Farrell needs is a little reforming. I'm only doing what any concerned parent would do if he suspected his son might be heading down the wrong road."

"Aren't you being a bit dramatic? Farrell isn't a criminal!"

"I'm not suggesting that he is—or that he's likely to be. I do think that without some guidance he could end up living a pretty useless life—and maybe a short one."

Irritated at his supremely confident tone, she said, "You are going to force him to rebel!"

"Because I care enough about what happens to him to spell out what I consider acceptable behavior?" His voice held condescending amusement. Before she had a chance to reply, he added, "Asudi knew you didn't have the conviction to stand up to Farrell, and that's why he gave me the job."

She hesitated, finding this argument unanswerable. Jordan was right about Asudi and his reason for not naming her Farrell's guardian. "I—I still think you might let up a bit," she said finally.

"The time to let up," said Jordan, "is after Farrell learns I'm calling the shots and that my expectations are in his best interest."

This effectively ended the discussion. Jordan lingered at the table over a final cup of coffee while Tiana helped Millie clear the table and finish in the kitchen. The housekeeper left at eight, reminding Tiana to unplug the half-full electric percolator before going to bed. Tiana assured her that she would and, left alone in the kitchen, poured herself another cup of coffee and gazed out the kitchen window, as she drank it, at the gathering darkness.

A few minutes later Jordan brought his empty cup into the kitchen. "We'll have the house to ourselves for a while," he said. "Would you like to play that game of backgammon we had to postpone the other night?" Noticing her hesitation, he added, "Or maybe you'd prefer a walk in the moonlight." He kneaded the muscles at the back of his neck. "A long walk would help me to unwind, I think."

72

She felt a creeping unease at the prospect of spending the evening alone with Jordan in the quiet house, but the idea of a moonlight walk was even more alarming.

He was watching her, his dark eyes half hidden by his lids. "Are you afraid to be alone with me?" he asked in a soft, yet scornful, voice.

She clenched her hands at her side, longing to hit him. "Don't be ridiculous."

"Then come for a walk," he said lightly.

"No—" she said quickly. "I have studying to do."

He gave her a long, measuring look before turning on his heel and leaving the house. She went back into her bedroom, leaving the light off and peering out the window to see Jordan strolling away from the house in the direction of the creek. When he was out of sight, she opened the sliding glass doors and stepped out on to the deck where, leaning against the redwood railing, she breathed deeply of the summer night. After a while she went back inside, closed the draperies, switched on the light, and turned the locks on both doors. Then she took a long, leisurely bath and got into her nightgown before opening the textbook to finish the reading assignment. More than an hour later she heard Jordan returning. He didn't call to her or come near her bedroom door. After a few minutes she heard voices from the living room and realized he had turned on the television set. At exactly ten twenty-seven she heard the jeep returning. When Farrell came in, he and Jordan talked briefly, but the words were indistinguishable. Then Farrell passed her door on the way to his own room.

Tiana turned out her light and went to bed, realizing that she had not really expected Farrell to comply with Jordan's curfew. He had never taken seriously any suggested by her or Asudi. She had thought he would, at least, miss the ten thirty deadline by a few minutes, just to show his displeasure. Instead, he had returned on time and had even exchanged what had seemed to be a few amiable words with Jordan before retiring.

Much as she disliked admitting it—because he was a man, because he was not so emotionally involved, or for whatever reason—Jordan seemed to know instinctively how to handle her brother.

5

By the following Saturday morning Tiana could admit, with a rueful smile, that Jordan's deftness in casting himself in the role of guardian-mentor-friend to Farrell had aroused in her a little plain and simple jealousy. Despite her predictions that Farrell would rebel against Jordan's rules, her brother seemed more accepting of his situation with each passing day. He had gone into town in Jordan's jeep again on Friday evening and, as on the previous occasion, had returned a few minutes before ten thirty.

Also, despite her apprehensions, Jordan had not suggested again that she join him in a moonlight stroll or, in fact, done anything in an effort to draw her into a more intimate relationship. He spent hours each day in his studio and treated her with a casual friendliness whenever they were together. It was, Tiana told herself, as if that passionate kiss in the kitchen had never happened. She did wonder wryly if he was merely biding his time until another such opportunity presented itself; but she quickly brushed this thought aside as being unfair to Jordan, who had evidently decided to take her at her word that she wanted him to keep his distance.

In fact, Jordan was behaving so circumspectly that when Tiana found herself with time on her hands in the evening, she was unable to bring herself to suggest even a backgammon game for fear of appearing to take too much for granted. Therefore, it was with a great deal of anticipation that she looked forward to her Saturday night date with Dale for dinner and a movie. Since both had eaten late lunches, they decided to see the movie first. It was, consequently, rather late by the time they claimed the table Dale had reserved at the recently renovated supper club on the outskirts of Tahlequah.

Dinner was delicious, filets smothered in mushrooms being the main course. After they had eaten, Dale led her onto the small dance floor and held her easily while they moved smoothly to the slow music. The evening with Dale had lulled Tiana back into placid contentment, but her feelings of peace were shattered when she looked over Dale's shoulder and saw Jordan standing in the arched entry to the dining room. Her first thought was that something had happened to Farrell and Jordan had come looking for her. She vaguely recalled mentioning to him where she and Dale were going.

However, she was mistaken about the reason for Jordan's appearance, a truth which was brought home to her when Lois Graham appeared in the archway beside Jordan and, taking his arm, walked with him to a corner table. By that time Tiana had had time to take in the handsomely tailored blue suit Jordan wore with a white shirt and tie and realize that he was there for a dinner date with Lois, who looked quite ravishing in a white silk figure-hugging dress with a neckline that plunged shockingly.

"Isn't that Jordan Ridge with Lois Graham?" asked Dale, following the direction of her look.

"Yes, it is," Tiana replied, glancing up at him to smile. She wondered why Jordan hadn't mentioned that he was seeing Lois. As far as Tiana knew, it was the first time since the previous Saturday evening when Lois had invaded his living room and, for some reason, Tiana had drawn the conclusion that Jordan's interest in the blonde was waning. Judging from their apparent engrossment in each other at the moment, though, that did not seem likely. Tiana felt a twinge at this, something very akin to disappointment.

"Small world isn't it?" commented Dale, still looking toward the corner table where Jordan and Lois were sitting.

"That woman sure doesn't hide anything, does she? I hear Ridge has been seeing her longer than any of the women before her."

"Do you?" Tiana made an offhand movement of her shoulders, not understanding her own reactions.

"Maybe he's going to marry her and give up his philandering ways. That's the scuttlebutt around town, anyway."

Tiana murmured something vague and noncommittal. She was glad when the song ended as she could suggest that they start home.

As they left the dance floor, she wondered if Jordan had seen her, but she didn't look toward his table again. In the car Dale seemed in no hurry to reach the house. Instead, he drove slowly along the highway, eventually turning onto the graveled road and pulling off to stop on a grassy bank alongside. Tiana had managed to shake off her depressed feeling during the drive and nestled contentedly against Dale's shoulder when he moved to put his arm around her. When he kissed her, however, Nancy's impertinent question popped into her head and, perversely, would not leave. She pulled away and Dale asked, "Is anything wrong?"

"No—" She moved a little away from him to rest her head on the back of the seat. "I'm just tired, I guess."

"Why didn't you go and speak to Ridge and his lady friend in the dining room?" he asked suddenly.

Tiana turned to peer at his profile in the dim moonlight. "I don't know. Why do you ask?"

He shrugged slightly. "It seemed odd to me. I mean you live with him and all."

"I didn't think they saw us," Tiana said lightly, "and I didn't want to intrude."

"It would simplify things if he'd marry her right away," Dale said, continuing with his own thoughts as if Tiana had not spoken.

"I don't understand what you're getting at," Tiana said, feeling herself tighten up inside. "Rumors may be flying, but I don't think Jordan has any intention of marrying

77

Lois—or anyone else. Not at the present, anyway—and I fail to see what would be simplified if he did."

"I'm thinking of you and your reputation."

"Oh." Tiana sighed heavily. "I thought we'd settled that."

"To your satisfaction, maybe," Dale retorted, "not mine. There is another solution, though."

"If you are going to suggest that I move out—" Tiana began.

"I'm not. I—" He reached suddenly for her hands, taking them into his own and turning her so that he could look directly into her eyes. Even in the shadowy dimness she could see the intensity in his face. "Will you marry me, Tiana? I'm not trying to rush you. I'm not even asking you to set a date right now. But if we were formally engaged . . ."

"Then I would be safely removed from the realm of speculation as far as Jordan's affairs are concerned?" Tiana finished sharply. "Dale, that's no reason to become engaged!"

"That's not the reason," he protested urgently, "not the main reason, anyway. Tiana, we could have a good marriage. We want the same things and we get along well together. I love you. You must know that!"

He loved her. But why had he mentioned all the other reasons first? There seemed something oddly wrong with that. "I—I don't know," she murmured unevenly. "You've taken me by surprise. You'll have to give me time to think about it, Dale."

He bent to kiss her lightly, then released her hands and started the car again. "All right. I won't press you. You think about it, but there isn't really all that much to think about. We will probably marry eventually anyway. We have an understanding. At least I thought we did. This situation you're in has just pushed us into it a little sooner."

As he pulled back onto the road, Tiana sank against the seat, feeling a vague resentment at his choice of words.

They were being pushed into marriage, were they? But she said nothing. She merely closed her eyes and tried to make some sense of her jumbled thoughts on the remainder of the drive, feeling more confused than she had ever been in her life before.

At the house she checked on Farrell and found him asleep in his bed. Knowing she would not be able to sleep herself, she went into the kitchen and put on the kettle for hot tea. She was having a second cup, which she had carried into the living room, when Jordan came in.

She looked up from the couch in surprise. "I didn't think you'd be back for hours. You must have rushed through dinner—" The words were out before she realized it, and she stammered to a halt.

"So you did see Lois and me at the supper club? Why didn't you come over and say hello?"

"Dale wanted to leave," she lied. "He'd had a long day and was tired."

"I see." He stood in front of the stone fireplace, looking down at her, their ancestors trudging despairingly through the snow in the painting behind him.

"I suspected you didn't care to introduce me to Dale." Jordan's expression seemed cold and forbidding.

"I can't imagine why you thought that! It was late and we both wanted to go home. Frankly, you never entered either of our minds."

Jordan nodded curtly and her eyes drifted from his, down the tall length of his body in the blue suit. Then, looking back at him, she noticed that his skin looked very dark against the snowy whiteness of his shirt.

"Tiana, what's going on behind that blank face of yours?"

The harshness of his voice brought her chin up with a snap, and she realized suddenly that he had been aware of her lingering appraisal. She saw a muscle tighten along one side of his mouth, and his cheekbones seemed suddenly to harden.

She got to her feet. "I—I'm going to bed."

"Yes," he said tightly, "I think that would be a good idea."

She walked out of the room on unsteady legs, and he watched her go without moving.

For the first time Jordan truly doubted the wisdom of having Tiana in his house. Outwardly, she was cool and collected, but he sensed that underneath that aloof exterior were deep wells of passion just waiting to be plumbed. One day the right man would come along, someone who could get past her defenses and . . .

But he was not that man, he told himself. Something warned him that a relationship with Tiana would not be casual or fleeting. She had told him in enough ways that she wouldn't settle for that. No, Tiana was the sort of woman who wanted a commitment, the sort of woman he had made it a policy to avoid. Maddening, but there it was. He had no intention of giving up his carefree life-style, not even for Asudi's beautiful granddaughter. It followed, therefore, that there could be nothing at all between them, and he might as well accept that with good grace.

Better to stick to Lois and her ilk. Yet, even as this thought ran through his mind, he regretted that he had called Lois at the last minute and made the dinner date. He hadn't intended to, but for some reason when Tiana had left with Dale Gregory, he'd felt irritable and bored thinking of spending the evening with Farrell, who was perfectly satisfied to lose himself in television viewing for hours at a stretch. So, on an impulse, he had called Lois and had regretted it almost as soon as he'd landed on her doorstep.

During dinner she had managed to drop in several intensely curious questions abojut Tiana: How long was she planning to stay at Jordan's? Didn't Jordan feel that she was imposing on his hospitality? He wasn't *her* guardian. When was she going to marry that vice-principal?

Jordan wondered suddenly what he'd ever seen in Lois and recognized in himself the feelings of dissatisfaction and restlessness that always preceded a break-up with a woman.

He grimaced at the realization. Breaking up with Lois wasn't a pleasant thing to anticipate. He was very much afraid that she believed he would eventually marry her. Not that he'd ever said or done anything to lead her to that conclusion, but he had been dating her a long time and he supposed he should have broken off with her months ago.

He wished, not for the first time, that two people could come to the conclusion simultaneously that their relationship had outlasted whatever combination of chemistry had brought it into being. Unfortunately, this was rarely the case. Nor was it in the present instance. During the next few weeks, just as Jordan had feared, Lois intensified her efforts to keep Jordan interested. She telephoned every day or two until finally he began to make excuses, through Millie or Farrell, not to come to the phone.

Tiana, of course, was aware of the apparent state of affairs between Jordan and Lois, but she was not particularly gratified to learn that Jordan seemed finally to have grown weary of Lois's rather obvious surface charms. Tiana's relationship with him was more strained than ever. The two of them had crossed swords several times during the past few weeks over his continued rigid strictures on Farrell's activities. On these occasions she had accused him of being too strict, and he had called her a pushover and said she had been far too lenient with Farrell in the past, which was what made it necessary to impose stringent measures now. These confrontations always ended in a draw, neither of the combatants being inclined to change his stance.

One evening in late June, after Jordan had given grudging permission for Farrell to take a girl to a late movie on a week night, Tiana's nerves, which had been particularly strained the past few days, snapped and she rounded on him.

"I don't see how Farrell can enjoy the evening with all the stipulations you placed on his freedom!"

"Of course he'll enjoy it," Jordan retorted. "He's young

81

and rather taken with that pretty little Valley girl. And I did extend his curfew an hour."

They were in the living room and he walked over to the couch and dropped onto it. He looked drained after a long day in his studio, but Tiana was in no mood to feel sympathetic.

"Oh, right!" she flared, walking far enough so that she could look into his face. "*After* you listed all the places he was not allowed to frequent. You even told him how to act!"

"I merely suggested that he go to the door to pick up his date and not sit in the jeep and honk for her. Farrell needs to learn a little respect."

"You're a fine one to be instructing seventeen-year-old boys in how to behave with girls! But then I suppose you subscribe to the do-as-I-say-not-as-I-do school."

Jordan, who had sunk back against the couch cushion and was running weary fingers through his hair, stiffened and glared up at her. He got to his feet slowly. "I'm damned tired of your insults, Tiana!"

The cold fury in his eyes caused her to feel a sudden flutter of panic, and she took a step back. He looked angry enough to shake her or . . . But she was not to know what he might have done, for at that moment the phone rang, jarring into the electric silence that had followed Jordan's last words.

With an explosive curse, he walked over to the phone and snatched up the receiver. "Yes?" In the slight pause that followed, his glance raked over Tiana imperiously. Then he said, "I know you've been trying to reach me, Lois. I've been busy."

Tiana took the opportunity to escape. She retreated to the kitchen and passed through the back door to the deck. Standing for a moment in the early evening stillness, she looked toward the woods where the trees were dark sentinels in the soft gray dusk. Recalling the days when she used to wander through those trees, soaking up the peace and quiet and watching Jordan from her hiding place, she wondered if she would ever find that same kind of serenity again. On impulse, she ran down the redwood steps and walked toward the woods. She was wearing lightweight slacks and a thin, sleeveless knit shirt, but she wouldn't be outside long. She would return to the house before the night-time coolness found its way to the woods.

By the time she had reached the trees, she was already beginning to regret her outburst in the living room. Jordan was doing what he thought was best for Farrell; she could not deny that. And, indeed, her brother did not seem to resent his guardian as much as he had at first. Oddly, it seemed that as Farrell's resentment had lessened, Tiana's had grown.

In all fairness, though, she couldn't blame Jordan entirely for the taut state of her nerves lately. Her classes at the university kept her scrambling to keep up with the outside assignments, and Dale had been pressing her for an answer to his proposal. To top everything off, she had spoken to Nancy Pearson about sharing her apartment in the fall and Nancy had begun trying to coax Tiana into moving in with her immediately. Not that Nancy meant to pressure her overmuch, it was just that Tiana hadn't been able to explain to her friend's satisfaction why she wouldn't leave Jordan's house until Farrell did.

It was Dale's increasing demands, however, that had her nerves tied in knots. The problem was that she simply could not seem to make up her mind. On the one hand, she really believed that Dale would be a perfect husband for her. They had interests in common. Neither of them was inclined to be possessive or unreasonably demanding of the other's attention. As Dale's wife she would be able to continue her teaching career and other interests as well, Dale was good-natured and amiable and a fine specimen of a man—strong, healthy, nice-looking. They should have attractive children.

Tiana kicked at a fallen twig at her feet and walked on, smiling as she recalled Nancy's reaction when she'd presented to her friend these various reasons why she ought to marry Dale.

"Sounds as though you're thinking of buying a stud horse for a bunch of mares instead of taking a husband for yourself," Nancy had commented.

Tiana sighed. It wasn't that she wanted to be madly in love with Dale, like some giddy adolescent. She had convinced herself that a sane, calm sort of love was the basis for a lasting marriage. So why couldn't she bring herself to say yes to Dale?

"Tiana . . ."

Jordan's voice behind her caused her to start violently and whirl around.

"Sorry, I didn't mean to frighten you."

The evening dusk had deepened in the woods and his face was partially in shadow. Yet she sensed that his eyes moved probingly over her. Shivering, more from his nearness than from the evening chill, she said, "I was lost in thought. I—I'd better go back to the house and help Millie finish up in the kitchen."

He moved into her path silently as she tried to pass him. The shadowy darkness of his eyes fastened on her as if, by the sheer force of his look, he meant to immobilize her. "Millie has already left."

Desperate to put distance between them, Tiana turned back to the path and walked away from him, deeper into the woods. With a few long strides he was beside her.

"Mind if I join you?"

What could she say? It would be the height of rudeness to refuse and, besides, it would probably give him the idea she was afraid to be alone with him. He'd already accused her of that.

They walked slowly, side by side. "Still angry with me?"

She looked over at him briefly. "Angry?"

"Because of Farrell."

She shook her head. "No. I think maybe I overreacted. I know you're trying to do what you think Grandfather

84

would want. I just hope it doesn't backfire on you. I've never known Farrell to accept restraints so docilely."

He shrugged carelessly. "I'll worry about that when it happens. I never cross bridges until I come to them—unlike you."

She came to a stop, peering up at him. "What do you mean by that?"

"Just that you don't like surprises." His tone sounded as if he didn't mean this observation as a compliment.

"Where Farrell is concerned . . ." she began.

Without warning, his arms encircled her slender body, effectively trapping her. "Let's forget about Farrell and Millie and everybody else for a while." She tried to move away, to break his hold on her.

But his grip tightened and the brooding darkness in his face transfixed her as if she were mesmerized. Her heart pounded erratically and she felt a rush of sensations against which she had fought for so long.

In a last desperate try to divert him, she asked shakily, "Even Lois?"

"Especially Lois," he replied, his piercing gaze holding her own. The feel and smell of him, the overpowering aura of masculinity drowned out the rational part of her mind. She waited helplessly as he lowered his face toward her.

In the weeks since that other kiss, she thought she had managed to push the memory aside. But now she found that she had not forgotten anything. There was the same bursting dam of emotions as his mouth tantalized hers, and she found that she was returning the kiss.

The seconds spun out as they kissed desperately, her arms finding their way to the back of his head to pull him even nearer, her slender body trembling in his arms. It was almost like fainting, she thought wildly, when all the bodily restraints let go. Even the pins that held her chignon in place had slipped out and she felt the heavy weight of her long hair falling about her shoulders. Jordan's strong fingers were entangled in the tresses and he groaned softly, deep in his throat, as his lips left hers to blaze a trail of fire down her cheek and settle warmly against her neck.

She felt hot, yet she was shivering, and one small corner of her brain warned her to free herself before it was too late. "Jordan, you must stop—" The words sounded breathless and frail. "There is something you must know." Her voice was growing a little stronger now, as reason began to assert itself. "Dale has asked me to marry him."

He raised his head and stared down at her with brooding stillness. "Forget Dale," he said harshly and her senses stirred at the jealousy she thought she detected in the tone. "Forget everything except you and me—and this." He pulled her against him ruthlessly, kissing her violently, his tongue tasting her lips and reawakening the ache inside her until it grew to a poignant, terrifying sweetness that was new to her.

"You're beautiful," he whispered huskily against her lips. "You should always let your hair be free like this. Let *yourself* be free, Tiana." His tone was urgent now. "You want me. I know you do."

She struggled to reach the lost ability to deny him. Gasping for breath, she pushed away the hand that had dropped to her breast and was caressing the warm fullness gently. "Stop," she quavered. "I don't want this. I—I'm in love with Dale. I—"

"You're lying," he said between his teeth. "You couldn't respond to me the way you do if you were in love with another man."

"Well, *this* isn't love," she said bitterly. "It's only a momentary weakness on my part, and I regret it already. Dale is kind and gentle and he—he respects me."

She felt his fingers digging into the soft skin of her arms and she struggled to be free. But her strength was no match for his, and he held her rigidly still. "Because he wants to marry you?" he asked scornfully. "Because he's willing to pay your price?" His mouth took hers again with angry ferocity, her body crushed against his hard, muscled chest and thighs. She twisted and turned in her attempts to escape, tasting the sharpness of her own blood as his mouth crushed her lips against her teeth. She felt suddenly dizzy and her resistance decreased. Jordan's kiss altered then, became gentle and seductive. His hands moved over her back, caressing the soft skin though the thin shirt, and his breathing was ragged.

Slowly, he lifted his mouth, looking at her with eyes which moved over her hungrily. "Forget all those school-girl notions of romance, Tiana. You're a woman now and the feelings you have are a woman's feelings. *This* is real—not those old-fashioned ideas you've filled your head with."

"Like love and marriage?" she asked bitterly, chilled by his words and still stung by the insinuation that her price for going to bed with Dale was marriage.

Jordan's face filled with harshness. "I want you, but I won't say things I don't mean. All that meaningless rubbish about hearts and flowers and undying love. I'm a man and you're a woman, and we have a strong sexual attraction for each other. I've wanted you for weeks now—so much that I can't sleep nights." His eyes burned down at her resentfully. "I've never been jealous before in my life, but the thought of Dale Gregory touching you makes me see red. If that gives you any satisfaction, you're welcome to it. But don't ask me to lie to you."

Trembling and stunned, Tiana backed away from him. "Thank you for being honest with me," she said tightly. "I'm not asking you for anything, Jordan. You don't have anything that I want. I almost forgot that for a few minutes there, but it won't happen again. Without meaning to, you've made me see what a wonderful man Dale Gregory really is."

He expelled a long, uneven breath. "Because he's willing to play your game? He wants to marry you to get you in bed, Tiana. You've managed to trap him, and because of that you think he's wonderful."

Her hand flew out and struck his mocking face. For a moment she stood there as if she were frozen, shocked at what she'd done, her hand still upraised, the palm stinging from the impact with his cheek. Then, her breath catching on a sob, she whirled and ran away from him.

By the time she had reached the house, she had managed to get a grip on her emotions. She went directly to the phone and called Dale, arranging to meet him in town for dessert and coffee. She had to get away for a little while and Dale sounded pleased at the thought of seeing her.

When she hung up, she went to her bedroom and pinned her hair back into its chignon. When she walked into the living room on her way out, Jordan was leaning against the fireplace, hands thrust deep into his pockets, almost as if he'd been waiting for her.

"Where are you going?" he demanded.

"Into town to meet Dale," she replied coolly, forcing herself to meet his taunting look. "Fortunately, *I* don't have a curfew."

His lips curved into a smile that did not touch his eyes. "Now that you're planning to marry the man, I'm sure the two of you have a lot to discuss. It must be inconvenient meeting in public places. Or have you overcome your maidenly qualms to the extent that you can go to his apartment? Well, in case you haven't, there's plenty of room here." His long arm swept out, encompassing the room in a magnanimous gesture. "Feel free to bring your boyfriend here whenever you want."

She looked back at him levelly without reply until, abruptly, he turned on his heel and left the room. As she let herself out, she heard the door of his studio slam shut behind him.

6

"This is an unexpected pleasure. You must have finished your homework sooner than you planned." Dale was facing Tiana across a table in the Tahlequah restaurant where they often met.

"I know I told you yesterday that I couldn't see you tonight because I had so much homework to do," Tiana responded. "I still have homework to do, I'm afraid. I just felt I had to get out of the house for a while."

He looked almost boyish in tight-fitting denim trousers and a yellow fishnet shirt, his sandy hair falling across his forehead carelessly. "Well, I'm glad you called. A few minutes earlier and I'd not have been there. I had a late afternoon golf game with Harris." He looked down at the fishnet shirt with slight embarrassment. "That's why I'm dressed so sloppily."

Tiana, who still wore the same slacks and knit shirt she'd donned that morning, said, "I'm not dressed for a night on the town myself. It doesn't matter."

"No," he breathed with some satisfaction, "it doesn't. The important thing is that we're here together." He reached across the table and squeezed her hand, which rested on the checkered cloth.

After a moment, Tiana disentangled her fingers, though it was nice to have Dale sitting across the table from her, so solid and frankly glad to see her.

"I—I was too restless to concentrate on child psychology," she murmured, smoothing her hair with a nervous hand.

"Did something happen to upset you?" he asked, immediately concerned.

"What?" Tiana's smile was tentative. "Oh, no—I only wanted to be with you for a bit."

"Good." He settled back in his chair with an easy smile. "It's nice to be appreciated."

They lingered for half an hour over apple pie à la mode and coffee, and, for the first time since her meeting in the woods with Jordan, Tiana relaxed.

"So." Dale put an arm around her as they left the restaurant together. "You were missing me, were you?"

"Yes," Tiana said lightly. "I must be getting used to having you around."

Outside, the street was almost deserted. They strolled slowly toward the curb where their cars were parked, side by side. Standing between the vehicles, Dale looked down at her. "I kind of like having you around, too, you know," and he bent his head to touch her mouth with his own.

Tiana felt her body stiffen. Her emotions had already been shredded once that evening, and she felt too drained to go through another upheaval of the senses. But his kiss was gentle and disarming and she found her lips parting in reluctant response. He murmured her name softly as his arms tightened around her, his hands sliding across her back to hold her closer.

She could feel his heart pounding heavily and sensed an uncommon urgency in him. For Tiana's part, the feeling that swept over her when he released her mouth to press his lips against her hair was mostly relief. He was being as eagerly affectionate as any girl could wish, yet there was no stunning assault on Tiana's senses. She had enjoyed the kiss well enough and the way his hands were stroking her back made her feel as contented as a cat. But there were no exploding emotions careening out of control, no feeling that she might lose her hold on reality. Whatever insanity had gripped her when Jordan held her in his arms had left her, and she was determined never to give way to that kind of out-of-control sensuality again.

After a few moments, she moved away from him and got into her car. Dale had bent to lean through the open window and give her another brief kiss on the cheek. They murmured their good-byes and Tiana turned the key in the ignition. Nothing happened.

"Oh, no!" she wailed, her heart sinking. "That's all I need. My car won't start." She turned the key again and elicited only a clicking sound.

Dale walked to the front of the car and opened the hood. "Do you have a flashlight?" he called to her.

She thrust her head out the window. "No. What do you think is wrong?"

He felt around under the hood for a few moments, then slammed it down and came back around to her window. "I think it's the battery. Come on, I'll take you home."

"Oh, but—" Tiana began uncertainly. "I can't leave my car here."

"It'll be all right until tomorrow," Dale assured her. "I'll get the mechanic who takes care of my car to look at it. The problem is probably a minor one."

Tiana agreed, not knowing what else to do. At least she didn't have classes the next day and perhaps the problem, whatever it was, could be taken care of before Friday. She got into Dale's car, giving him the key to hers. "Tell him to call me before he does anything expensive."

He pulled into the street and Tiana let her head fall back against the seat with weary resignation. This definitely wasn't her day. Dale took her hand, holding it loosely on the seat between them.

"Don't worry about it," he said soothingly.

She turned her head to smile at him. "Okay." But that didn't keep her from mentally rearranging her budget to accommodate an unexpected car repair. It wasn't easy to fit in unplanned expenses.

"You fret too much about things that can't be helped," Dale said after a moment.

His words brought back Jordan's statement when they had been in the woods together: *You don't like surprises.*

91

Well, maybe she was a bit uptight about such things. What was it Nancy always said? Think of the worst thing that could happen and what you'd do about it, and you'll realize things are usually not as bad as they seem.

The worst thing that could happen is that her car could be too far gone to salvage. If *that* happened, she could always move into town with Nancy and walk to her classes. It really wouldn't be the end of the world.

"I'll forget the car until I hear from you—or that mechanic," she said decisively.

"Good girl." He squeezed her hand and gave her an approving glance.

When they reached the house, the lights were on in the living room and, on a sudden impulse, Tiana suggested, "Why don't you come in for a while? I'll make some tea."

"Are you sure it's all right?"

Remembering Jordan's suggestion that she invite Dale to the house which, now that she'd had time to reflect upon it, had sounded decidedly challenging, Tiana said promptly, "Absolutely."

"What about your homework?"

She suspected that, for some reason, he was reluctant to meet Jordan on the artist's home ground. "I'll do it tomorrow," she said. It suddenly seemed important that Dale come inside with her, just to show Jordan . . . Show him what? Well, she'd figure that one out later.

When they entered the living room, Jordan was sprawled on the couch studying some pencil sketches in a drawing tablet. He looked up abstractedly when he heard them, then put the tablet aside, his eyes taking in the intruders. His expression was unreadable, and Tiana began to wonder if it had been wise, insisting that Dale come inside. But there was nothing to do now but to brazen it out. She made the introductions and, at Jordan's invitation, Dale sat down on the opposite end of the couch.

Tiana said rather defiantly, "I'm going to make Dale some hot tea. Would you care for a cup, Jordan?" Surely he would excuse himself and leave them alone.

But, no, he said carelessly, "Yes, thank you."

Tiana was reluctant to leave them alone, even for the few minutes it would take to brew the tea, but there was no helping it. She gave Dale a reassuring smile. "I'll be right back."

As she left the room, she heard Dale saying, "I heard that you'll be exhibiting some of your paintings in Paris soon," and she felt relieved. Maybe they would discuss Jordan's work until she returned.

She prepared the tea as quickly as she could, poured three cups and arranged them on a tray with spoons, cream, and sugar. As she carried the tray into the living room, Jordan remarked, "You didn't tell me that Dale has Cherokee blood, Tiana."

She set the tray on the coffee table in front of the couch. "It—it never came up. I forget it myself sometimes." She glanced at Dale as she handed him his cup and offered cream and sugar.

"Actually, I'm part Creek, too, but I never had much contact with my Indian relations. They're on my mother's side, and I think there are some hard feelings over something that happened years ago. I never really felt any ties with my Indianness, I guess."

Jordan was nodding his head rather thoughtfully as he spooned sugar into his tea. "Your coloring doesn't show it, certainly. Perhaps you feel that is just as well. Being Indian is not an asset in some quarters." His tone was good-humored and lightly mocking, and Tiana felt her ire kindling. What was he trying to do, draw Dale into an argument?

In fact, she realized that she resented Jordan's talking to Dale at all. What irritated her most, however, was the ease with which Jordan slouched back against the couch and sipped his tea, as if he fully intended staying there all night.

Dale's expression had hardened slightly as he perhaps suspected that Jordan was baiting him. "I'm no bigot," he said rather testily. "I just don't think a person's ancestry is all that important." He glanced at Tiana and smiled uncomfortably. "We're all Americans, aren't we?"

He sounded suddenly rather pompous and shallow to Tiana, but she put this feeling down to her own tiredness. She sat down beside Dale and slipped her hand through the crook of his elbow, resting her fingers lightly on his forearm. When she glanced Jordan's way, she saw the sardonic amusement in his darkening eyes.

"On the other hand," Jordan drawled deliberately, "some of us take a great deal of pride in heritage and tradition. Tiana's grandfather, for example, brought her up to revere the glorious Cherokee past. Isn't that right, Tiana?"

Tiana felt her jaw quivering. "Dale never even met my grandfather, and I'm sure he's not interested in how I was raised." She was irritated beyond all reason at her inability to comprehend her own feelings.

"So you never met Asudi?" Jordan went on. "I'm surprised." His voice was level, but one eyebrow rose quizzically, and Tiana shot a furious glance in his direction.

"Why should you be?" she declared, pressing closer to Dale. "Grandfather rarely left the farm." She sounded stupid and childish, and she knew it.

"I merely assumed," Jordan returned, settling ever more comfortably into his lounging position, "that Dale must have been at the farm a number of times. Farrell told me that the two of you have been seeing each other for a good long while."

"We—why—" she mumbled, her cheeks hot. Had he actually been quizzing Farrell about Dale? "We always found it more convenient to meet in town."

Dale fidgeted nervously beside her and, finishing his tea, placed the cup on the coffee table.

Jordan said, "I see," and sipped his own tea slowly. His claiming Farrell as his informant was deliberate, she was sure, creating the impression that Tiana herself had told him nothing about her relationship with Dale. That, of course, was totally untrue.

Fortunately, Dale seemed not to notice. "Tiana and I

have been seeing each other for some time. Long enough to feel practically like·an old married couple already," he said complacently, patting Tiana's hand and smiling at her. This description somehow made their relationship sound mundane and unexciting. One glance at Jordan's slight smirk told Tiana that he was thinking the same thing.

There was a brief pause while Jordan continued to sip his tea and study them over the rim of the cup. Then he remarked, "It's too bad you didn't get to know Asudi. He was one of the most interesting conversationalists I've ever known."

Dale said uncertainly, "I'm sure." Then, in a rush of words, "I think I'd better head back to town, Tiana."

Before Jordan could come up with another two-edged comment, Tiana said quickly, "I'll see you to your car."

Dale seemed as relieved as she to leave the presence of the lounging man in the living room. Outside, he surprised Tiana by turning to her and demanding, "What's been going on out here, anyway?"

It was too dark to see his face clearly, but she didn't have to see him to sense that he was angry. "What are you talking about?"

"You and Ridge," he said tensely. "Is something going on between the two of you?"

"That is absolutely the most preposterous thing you've ever said to me!" Tiana exploded. "How can you even think—why, he's the most pompous, arrogant man I've ever known!"

"You're not falling for that Romeo, are you?"

"Stop this!" Tiana cried, angered almost to the point of tears. "I don't know what brought this on."

He was silent for a long moment, then he put his arms around her and she felt the tenseness easing out of him. "I'm sorry. It's only that I kept getting the feeling in there that something was going on below the surface. As if everything he said had one meaning for me and another for you—as if he meant it that way."

She pressed close to him, seeking comfort. "He's just a

95

very infuriating, egotistical man and I don't want to waste any more time even thinking about him."

"Neither do I," he agreed and kissed her with a swiftness that took her by surprise. The kiss was unlike his previous kisses—harder, more passionate—and Tiana did not really like it. His hand found its way beneath her shirt and slid warmly across the bare skin of her back. She pulled away from him, disconcerted.

"Ah, Tiana," he said huskily, "say you'll marry me soon."

Tiana licked her lips. "You—you promised not to press me . . ." A feeling akin to panic rose in her as she realized that, far from losing control of her senses with Dale, she was feeling something very like aversion to the thought of deeper intimacies with him.

"All right," he said with decided impatience, "but a man can stand only so much, Tiana." He let her go and she hugged herself, shivering a little.

"I'll call you tomorrow—about your car," he said as he walked toward the driveway. "Good night." With that, he got into his car and drove away.

Returning to the living room, she found Jordan still sprawled on the couch. One black eyebrow rose insolently. "No lingering good-byes?"

She stood in the center of the room, still angry over the way he had behaved. "That was the rudest display of manners I have ever seen!"

"Yes, he did leave abruptly, didn't he? And after you were so hospitable, too. It was—"

She cut him off. "I'm talking about *your* manners!"

"I thought I showed remarkable restraint, myself," he drawled.

"You—you're impossible!"

"Oh, come on, Tiana." He heaved an impatient breath. "Stop playing the role of the woman wronged. Your boyfriend didn't come off very well and you're looking for someone to blame."

"Well, I don't have to look very far, do I? *You* made him feel uncomfortable and out of place."

"He *was* out of place," he said flatly.

Unable to think of a sufficiently insulting reply, she clenched her fists and stalked out of the room, down the hall, and into her bedroom where she slammed the door with a furious flourish.

A long, hot bubble bath eased some of the tension. Jordan had been deliberately trying to alienate Dale and irritate her, she told herself. Somehow she thought that tomorrow he would be expecting her to renew the battle. It appeared that he got some kind of perverse pleasure out of infuriating her. Well, she wouldn't give him the satisfaction. Tomorrow she would be calm and aloof—as aloof as he was.

While she was still in the tub, she heard Farrell come in and go to bed. One thing she would have to give Jordan, she admitted; he was making her brother toe the line. She realized abruptly that since they had moved in with Jordan she hadn't spent a single night walking the floor, wondering where Farrell was and when he would be home. She smiled grimly to herself; every cloud had its silver lining, it seemed.

She stepped out of the tub, toweled herself, and got into a short lace-trimmed white nightgown. Her room felt stuffy, in spite of the air conditioning, and she opened the sliding glass doors to let in a little fresh air. Drawn by the hum of crickets and the far-off croaking of a frog, she moved out onto the deck and leaned on the railing, breathing in the fresh fragrance of cedar and elm and the lovely odor of the honeysuckle vine that climbed over a trellis near the house.

She brushed her long hair out, and it fell about her shoulders like a swathe of fine silk; and she felt much more relaxed after her bath. She stared at the trees at the edge of the yard, remembering that lonely section of the woods, the trees crowding all around like guardians, where Jordan had forced her senses to respond to him.

She closed her eyes, sighing raggedly. She was going to have to give Dale an answer to his proposal soon. After tonight she had serious doubts about whether it would be fair to Dale to marry him, knowing that Jordan could make her feel things that Dale, as her husband, never would. How could she swear to love, honor, and be true to Dale when she had weakened so easily under Jordan's attack? But, even more vital, she must manage to avoid being alone with Jordan as much as possible until she and Farrell could leave this house. She was no longer sure that she had the strength of will to deny her treacherous body where Jordan was concerned. Only a few weeks ago she would have sworn she could resist any man, a confidence that had proven to be childishly naive.

She was so lost in her tangled thoughts that she did not hear the movement beside her until Jordan was at her side. She whirled about, too startled to speak. He wore a light-colored terry robe which fell to the knees, and below that his legs were bare. He must have just bathed, too, for he smelled faintly of soap.

There was enough light from the open doors of her bedroom to see that his dark eyes were moving over her with hungry intensity. She was aware belatedly that she had not even put on a robe over her scanty nightgown. A wisp of breeze lifted the fragile lace slightly and set it aflutter like her heart.

Looking from him, she said, "I'll go in—"

"No. I want to talk to you." Somehow he had placed himself between her and the bedroom door, and she did not know whether to try to go around him, demand that he move, or talk and wait for a chance to escape.

"Say what you have to say then. It's getting cold out here." She was amazed at how steady her voice sounded, while inwardly she fought to still a whirlpool of churning emotions.

"How long are you going to keep Dale Gregory on the string?"

"I—I don't see that that's any concern of yours," she

said haughtily. "What right have you to question me about my personal life?"

"You don't love him," he said flatly, imperiously. He had moved so close to her that her back was pressing against the redwood railing.

She looked up at him, her eyes blazing. "You can't know that! What makes you think you know the first thing about how I feel? I happen to be very fond of Dale."

Staring down at her broodingly, he said, "I watched you cuddling next to him on the couch—the way you were touching him. You were playing up to him to get back at me. That's a cheap female trick, Tiana. Somehow I thought you were above that sort of thing."

"*You* thought!" she flared. "Well, do you want to know something? I don't *care* what you thought. Oh, you're a fine one to talk! You've made a career of leading women on! You've got Lois Graham calling here every day, poor deluded woman. And now you want me to break off with Dale—I suppose so that I will fall into your arms. How many women do you need at one time to satisfy your ego!"

The long, lean body that was almost touching her own stiffened. "You're jealous of Lois," he said harshly.

"I'm not!" Her voice broke on the words.

He made a sound that was half sigh and half growl as his fingers gripped her upper arms and hauled her against him. "Yes, you are. That's why you disliked Lois the moment you met her."

Soundlessly, she shook her head and stared into his eyes, feeling a helpless weakness creeping over her.

"I want to kiss you, Tiana," he said softly, "and you want it, too, don't you?"

Again, she shook her head, unable to speak. She felt sure she would have been unable to stand if he had not been holding her upright with his hands. Slowly, his head came down and she did not even turn her face away. His lips brushed hers with such tantalizing gentleness that she felt an anticipatory shiver run along all her nerves.

"Admit it, Tiana," he whispered. "You like it when I kiss you, don't you?"

"Y-yes," she admitted in resentful helplessness. She had played a part with Dale tonight, talking, smiling, pretending to be on the verge of falling in love with him, when all the time, in the back of her mind, had been the memory of Jordan's kisses. Jordan was right, she thought confusedly, she had played up to Dale in an attempt to make Jordan jealous. Only moments ago she had told herself that she would not let Jordan get close to her again—yet now she could no more stop her lips from responding to his languorous, seductive kiss than she could change herself into another person. Too long she had denied the deep recesses of her passions, and now every cell in her body seemed to be clamoring for fulfillment.

Jordan picked her up in his arms easily, as if she were a small child, and the white lace along the hem of her gown was outlined against the golden skin of her thighs as he walked through the open doors and laid her down on the bed. The room spun, and she felt dazed as she looked up at him and watched him lie down beside her with eyes that smoldered with dark passion.

His gaze traveled the length of her body and came to rest on her face. "Tonight when you were smiling at Dale and touching him, I wanted to throw him out. I wanted you to touch me and smile at me. I wanted to be alone with you like this."

"We—you mustn't do this . . ." she managed to get out while her senses were drowning with his nearness.

He laughed shortly, without humor. "Because you are engaged to Gregory? The two of you are like an old married couple, he said. What did he mean by that, Tiana? Have you—?"

"You have no right to ask me that," she retorted, angered by the peremptory tone of his voice. "You of all people have no right to question what others might have done in the past."

The cutting words made him rigid for a few seconds,

and then a knowing smile curved his mouth. Tiana felt a tremor of fear as she saw the predatory gleam in his eyes. His body pressed her back against the bed, his hand exploring the soft contours of her half-exposed breasts, his lips finding secret, sensitive spots on her neck and shoulders. She closed her eyes and tried to fight down the feeling that her very bones were melting. No man had ever touched her like this, made her feel so weak and unresisting. The tormenting sweetness terrified her.

Trying to catch her breath, she pushed his hand away.

"I'm tired of games, Tiana," he said warningly, and his moist tongue began to trace the outline of her breast. For just a moment she let herself lie still and feel the tender riot of her senses. A soft moan escaped her. Dimly, a new, frightening realization pushed into her consciousness. She loved this man. She had loved him for a long time, perhaps she had started to love him years ago when she used to watch him from the wooded hillside. Had even Edward been only a substitute for the unattainable Cherokee painter?

"Ah, Tiana . . ." The words were murmured with such yearning that they seemed almost to be torn from his throat against his will. "My beautiful Tiana. You know you want me as much as I want you."

She felt hot tears beneath her closed eyelids. "Jordan, if only——" She stopped, turning her face away from him.

His strong fingers gripped her chin, forced her to look into his face. "What, Tiana? Say it. At least be honest with me."

She swallowed convulsively and a single tear trickled down her cheek. "If I thought you loved me . . ."

He became very still, and his black brows drew together in a frown. "Tiana," he said haltingly, "love is only a word. You're a beautiful woman and I find you physically attractive. Our bodies react to each other in a fantastic way."

The words laid out with the precision of a measuring rod chilled Tiana. "Like animals," she whispered, the pain in her heart stabbing achingly. "From your viewpoint, Jordan, I could be any reasonably attractive woman. Lois Graham—or any number of others would do as well."

"No." He shook his head. "Whether you believe it or not, the tales of my conquests have been highly exaggerated. Painting is the most important thing in my life. There is no room for a wife and obligations. Oh, I've had relationships with women. But I haven't thought about any other woman for weeks now except you. I won't make empty promises, but I've never wanted a woman the way I want you."

She sighed, feeling such anguish. "That is only because I am harder to get than some, I think. Yes, Jordan, I want you—I admit it—but not this way. You can rape me, but that is the only way you will have me."

He stared down at her, an angry scowl sharpening his features. "Don't be such a little fool!" He entangled his fingers in her hair, holding her head still, and began to kiss her again—fiercely, possessively. She lay still beneath him, summoning all the strength of her will not to respond. But the feelings were there, deep down inside her and, for a moment, she almost gave in, thinking that surely to have Jordan under whatever terms was better than not to have him at all. But some fragment of pride made her hold on to her control.

Finally, he lifted his head and looked at her with torment in his eyes. "You've gone as stiff as an ice maiden."

"Go away and leave me alone," she said forlornly.

He was silent for a moment, but he did not move. Finally, huskily, he said, "I want to take you to Paris with me in the fall. I have never taken a woman on an exhibiting tour, Tiana. I never wanted to before."

Sadly, she shook her head. "Oh, Jordan . . . do you think you can buy me with trips and things—l-like a kept woman? I may not feel the same things with Dale, but he can give me something you wouldn't understand—love and commitment."

She watched as rage flared his nostrils and made her pupils look as hard as onyx. She made herself meet his furious gaze without wavering. Somehow it was easier to deal with his anger than with his tenderness.

He swore violently, getting to his feet. "My God, you're as calculating as any other woman!" His face twisted with humiliation and bitterness. "Go ahead and marry that small-minded, pinch-souled, sorry excuse for a man! Marry him, Tiana, and you will regret it the rest of your life!"

His hands shook as they tugged at the belt of his robe, and he sent a glance of cold contempt over her body before he turned and walked out of the room.

Tiana lay unmoving for a long moment until, at last, her body began to tremble violently and the tears she had been holding back burst forth in shuddering, anguished sobs. She felt that she must surely be doomed to a life of utter misery, for she had done what she had vowed never to do. She had fallen hopelessly in love with Jordan—a man who did not even believe in love.

"Farrell, if you'd gotten up when your alarm went off, you wouldn't have to shovel in your breakfast like that." Tiana was placing two more pancakes on her brother's plate.

Millie turned from the stove to survey the boy. "You take your time and finish your breakfast, Farrell. It's not going to hurt anything if you're five minutes late getting started."

Tiana poured herself a cup of coffee and sat down at the table. "Didn't you finish painting the house trim yesterday?"

Farrell nodded as he drowned his pancakes in more maple syrup. "Jordan wants me to start fencing the new pasture for the horses today." He looked at Millie. "Did the lumber yard deliver the wire and posts?"

"They did." The housekeeper spotted his empty glass and, getting a pitcher of milk from the refrigerator, refilled it. "I had 'em unload it down by the creek where you told me." She straightened and said severely, "Slow down, son. Fencing is hard work, and if you don't start chewing before you swallow, you're going to have a bad case of indigestion."

Farrell ate only slightly more slowly, washing down the food with gulps of milk. After a moment, he paused to say earnestly, "I don't want to be late. I don't want to do anything to get Jordan's back up. He might decide I can't go to the Fourth of July party my friends are having."

"What's this about a Fourth of July party?" Jordan strode into the kitchen, his black hair still damp from his morning shower. He sat down beside Tiana, and Millie bustled about, pouring his coffee and carrying it to him, then pouring more pancake batter onto the hot griddle.

"My friends and I are planning to go over to Lake Gibson for the day," Farrell replied. "We're going to swim and have a picnic, and George Hickson thinks he can use his uncle's boat for water-skiing."

Jordan remained silent while he stirred cream into his coffee.

Eyeing him warily, Farrell added, "Half my graduating class will be there. It'll be the first time I've seen most of them since school was out."

"Will George Hickson's uncle be on hand to keep an eye on his boat?" Jordan asked.

"I—I think so," Farrell said hesitantly, "but even if he isn't, George knows how to handle it."

"I'd like to be assured," said Jordan, "that there will be a level head around to keep things from getting out of hand."

Farrell groaned. "You're acting like we're twelve years old. We haven't had chaperones at our parties for a couple of years now."

"Yes, Jordan," Tiana put in, unable to restrain her impatience. "Most of these kids are eighteen. Aren't you being a bit Victorian?" She relished the opportunity of applying the same appellation to him that he had once used to describe her.

Jordan glanced at Tiana briefly and suddenly the passionate scene in her bedroom the previous night flashed into her mind, causing her to look away in embarrassment. Then Jordan said to Farrell, "We'll discuss it later. Isn't it time for you to get to work now?"

"Oh, yeah." Farrell finished his milk and left the table with a final look of appeal thrown Tiana's way.

Millie placed Jordan's pancakes in front of him. The sound of the front door closing behind Farrell reached them. "That boy *has* been towing the mark, Jordan," Mil-

106

lie ventured. "Seems to me you ought to give him a little more rope."

"I agree," said Tiana quickly.

Jordan calmly buttered his pancakes and poured syrup over them. "If I'm too harsh, it's because I'm trying to deal with a lifetime of overindulgence."

Tiana seethed at the aspersion cast her way and was about to retort angrily when Millie cocked her head and said, "Listen, I think I hear Duke scratching at the back door. I'd better take him something to eat."

She filled a pan with the dry dog food from the pantry and went out through the dining area to the deck.

When Millie was out of earshot, Tiana said, "You are going to let Farrell go to the party, aren't you?"

"Someone's bound to bring alcohol," Jordan retorted shortly.

Tiana clenched her hands in her lap. "If Farrell wants to drink, he doesn't have to go to a party to do it!"

"Nevertheless," he replied imperturbably, "I see no reason to encourage him in that direction."

Tiana pushed her chair back, scraping it loudly across the tile floor, and got to her feet. "You're absolutely unreasonable," she flared. "Oh, I hate having to stay here and eat your food and . . . and feel that Farrell and I are becoming more obligated to you every day."

"I've told you there is no need for you to feel any obligation," he said, staring at her.

"I don't care! I just wish there was some way I could pay you back. What Millie gives me to do is hardly more than a token."

His expression was thoughtful. "Are you really serious about wanting to repay me?"

"You know I am," she retorted.

"Very well. I know of something you can do."

She looked into his steady eyes and asked cautiously, "What?"

"Pose for me."

107

She stared at him for a moment. "Pose . . . you mean you want to paint me?"

"Yes. I've been looking for something different from my usual subjects to add to the collection for the Paris exhibit. I haven't done many individual portraits and I'd like to do yours."

"But I'm not a model. I've never done anything like that before." Her eyes narrowed suspiciously. "If you think for one minute that I'd pose—unclothed—"

Jordan laughed shortly. "I know better than to push my luck *that* far." He continued to look at her. "Well, what do you say? You don't have classes today. We could start right away."

"I—I have to check on my car and I still have class assignments to do for tomorrow." Tiana's mind raced frantically, searching for a way out of this dilemma which her tongue had gotten her into.

"We can start this afternoon," Jordan went on, a challenge sparking in his dark eyes. "That is, if you really meant what you said."

Tiana knew when she was defeated. "All right. I think I can be free by then."

"Good." He turned his attention to his pancakes again as Millie re-entered the kitchen.

Tiana walked to the stove and poured herself another cup of coffee. "I'm going to my room to do some studying, Millie. Unless you need me here."

"You go on," Millie said unhesitatingly. "How many times do I have to tell you I've been running this house alone for more than five years?"

Tiana started for the door, carrying her coffee, but Jordan's voice stopped her before she crossed the threshold. "Come to my studio at two. Leave your hair down and wear that simple white tunic you wore to class yesterday."

Tiana murmured assent and went to her room, already dreading the long hours alone with Jordan in his studio. But she was unable to blame anyone but herself for her predicament. Why had she gone on about repaying him until he had finally called her bluff?

Later in the morning, Dale called to inform her that the mechanic had installed a new battery in her car and, while he thought it also needed a new alternator, he felt she could drive it awhile yet before having to spend any more money on it.

Millie drove her into town so that she could pay the mechanic for the battery and take her car back to Jordan's. Then Tiana helped Millie with lunch and got in another hour of reading before her two o'clock appointment to pose for Jordan. She'd brushed her hair out and changed into the low-necked white tunic with green slacks. When she knocked on the closed studio door, Jordan called out, "Come in."

She stepped inside, looking about curiously. This was the first time she'd been in the studio and she hadn't known quite what to expect. It was almost a disappointment to see that it was merely a large, light-flooded room with three walls made almost entirely of glass and the other painted white. The floor was covered with light-colored square tiles, and the only pieces of furniture were a dressing screen in one corner, a plain wooden chair, a chaise longue covered in a blue fabric, and the stool on wheels where Jordan sat, his easel facing him. Canvases were stacked against the painted wall, face in, and above the canvases ran a shelf on which lay many varieties of brushes, tubes, and pots of paint. A small utilitarian bathroom could be reached by the door at one end of the interior wall.

Jordan put aside the pencil with which he had been sketching and, getting to his feet, came toward her.

"I—I wasn't sure about these slacks," Tiana said uncertainly. "I mean the color may not be right."

His gaze swept over her. "It doesn't matter. I think I'm going to do you only from the waist up." He walked around her slowly, studying her, she thought indignantly, as if she were a chair—or a horse. Then he murmured something unintelligible and came to a stop in front of her, his eyes resting in the most disconcerting way, on her breasts.

"Take off the bra," he said curtly.

"What!" Heat invaded her cheeks and her eyes flew wide.

He ran an impatient hand through his hair. "Don't be such a prude! I want a more natural line. You can step behind the screen."

Tiana wavered in an agony of indecision, trying to deduce, from his scowling face, the real motive behind his request. Finally, he put a hand in the small of her back and pushed her toward the screen. "You're wasting my time."

Realizing the futility of arguing, she stepped behind the screen, removed her bra, and got back into her tunic. Undecided about what to do with the bra, she finally left it lying on the floor behind the screen and came out.

"Let's try the chaise longue," Jordan said, clearly eager to get on with the afternoon's work. She sat unresisting while he moved her limbs about as if she were a rag doll. Finally, he seemed satisfied with a half-reclining position and began to arrange her hair so that it fanned across one shoulder. At last he stepped back and studied her silently. Then he said, "That's good. Now try not to move too much." He stepped to his easel, put a clean piece of heavy paper in the clips at the top of the easel and, eyes narrowed, began to sketch.

Tiana was soon disabused of any notion that he might be considering mixing seduction with work. He seemed totally engrossed in what he was doing and hardly spoke to her at all except to caution her when she moved.

At the end of two hours, he said, "That's enough for today. I'll start preparing the canvas, but I don't need you for that."

She ached all over from having remained in the same position so long. Groaning, she got to her feet and stretched slowly. "I don't think I could have stood it another minute."

He smiled at her, the intense concentration slowly easing out of his face. "I knew I'd worked you to the limit. Thanks for being so patient." He lifted his shoulders and rolled his head back to ease cramped muscles. "If you have some free time Saturday, we'll have another session."

"All right," she agreed. Her suspicion of his motives had left her entirely during the afternoon and now she was glad to be able to do this quite simple thing in return for his hospitality.

"I know it isn't much," she added impulsively, "but I'll try to be available to pose for you whenever you want."

"Evidently you don't know what professional artists' models are paid," he returned with a wry lift of his brows. "Believe me, you'll be repaying me in full."

He seemed to be perfectly serious, and she said, "Good. I—I'll see you at dinner then." She turned to go.

"Aren't you forgetting something?"

She turned back to discover a teasing smile lurking about his lips. With a nod of his head, he indicated the article of clothing she had left lying on the floor beneath the screen. It had been visible, from where he sat, all afternoon.

She flushed furiously. "Oh, yes." Scooping up the offending article, she rolled it into a tight ball which could be concealed in her hands and left the studio, feeling Jordan's amused scrutiny like a hot branding iron on her back.

After that, Tiana posed on Tuesday and Thursday afternoons and sometimes for two or three hours on Saturdays. As the sessions came and went, she grew more and more curious to see the portrait, but Jordan refused to allow it, saying he never showed his paintings until he was finished with them.

One afternoon, after the session was finished, he did show her several of the paintings which were stacked against the wall—paintings that would be included in the Paris show. One of these was an impressionistic oil of Indianlike Little People dancing at the bottom of a lake. The

111

scene was viewed as if through still water, and the effect was striking.

"It's Grandfather's story," she breathed, and she felt anew a deep pang of loss inside her.

"Yes, I told you I wanted to paint it. Do you like it?"

She nodded, her throat suddenly too tight to speak for a moment.

"I'm glad." The response was sincere, as if her approval was actually of some importance to him.

He showed her several other paintings. His style had changed considerably from the early traditional Indian style that characterized "The Trial of Tears" which hung over the fireplace. These were much more impressionistic, and one was quite realistic. "Sometimes a subject seems inherently to call for a particular style," he explained and she nodded, not quite sure what he meant but determined not to admit it.

The Fourth of July fell on a Friday, and on Tuesday of that week, Jordan finally said that Farrell could attend the party at Lake Gibson, even agreeing to let him use the jeep to get there. This permission was granted after a long, private discussion with Farrell. Farrell was even more diligent in his fence-building on Wednesday and Thursday, clearly determined not to give Jordan the slightest reason to change his mind.

On Thursday night, Farrell went out to the garage to check the jeep and discovered that it wouldn't start. By that time, no mechanic could be found who would come out until after the Fourth. Farrell and Jordan spent more than two hours tinkering with the machine, to no avail. They came back to the house grease-streaked and tired, and Tiana did not think she had ever seen Farrell look so dejected.

"That old crate has been running on borrowed time for the last year," Jordan said resignedly. "It's going to take a complete overhaul to get it going again."

"Farrell can take my car," Tiana offered, "if *it* will

start." She was not at all sure that it would, for it had been extremely undependable for the past several days. Farrell went immediately to try it and came back shortly to report that the motor wouldn't even turn over.

"Well, that does it," Tiana said unhappily. "I'll have to get a new alternator first thing Monday. I'll have it towed in—and maybe Millie will loan me her car for Monday's classes."

"Well, this is just great!" Farrell's temper finally burst its bounds. "Now the only way I have to get to the lake is to hitchhike."

Jordan, who had started toward the bathroom to wash up, turned back to say emphatically, "Hitchhiking is out, Farrell. I won't allow it. Understand?"

Farrell glared mutinously from beneath his shaggy hair, but he said nothing and Jordan left the room without further comment.

"It wouldn't hurt him to let me use his precious Jag," Farrell snarled and threw himself onto the sofa.

"You know that isn't likely to happen," Tiana told him. "That car is too low to be driven over those lake roads, anyway."

Farrell cursed darkly, and Tiana sat down beside him for a moment to pat his shoulder. "We can swim and have a picnic here."

"Fine!" he exploded. "While my friends enjoy the biggest bash of the summer!"

"I'm sorry, honey," Tiana said cajolingly, "but it can't be helped. Nobody could have foreseen that we'd have two cars out of commission." She touched his cheek lightly. "Come on, cheer up."

He jerked away from her. "Leave me alone!" he muttered as he stomped out of the room, leaving Tiana to wonder uneasily what was going through his mind.

She was not to discover the answer to this until Friday afternoon. Farrell had left the house after lunch, saying that he was going to take Duke for a walk. About an hour

113

later, Millie mentioned to Tiana that Duke had returned and was asleep on the deck, and she wondered where Farrell was.

"Probably sitting on a rock in the woods somewhere, feeling sorry for himself," Tiana said.

"It's a shame," Millie commented, "that he couldn't be with his friends today. Young people need to be with other young people."

Tiana nodded agreement, thinking that Farrell had taken his disappointment with remarkable stoicism, after that first burst of angry words. Her brother was, it seemed, maturing under Jordan's guardianship. He tackled whatever work Jordan gave him without complaint and clearly felt a great deal of satisfaction when he received his weekly paycheck. To Tiana's pleasure, he had opened a savings account in a Tahlequah bank and had deposited most of his earnings there.

About three, Jordan came out of his studio, finding Tiana and Millie having iced tea at the kitchen table.

"Where's Farrell?" he inquired.

"In the woods somewhere," Tiana said, frowning a little. "He's been gone an awfully long time, too."

"I've been thinking," Jordan said slowly. "I've decided to drive him over to Lake Gibson and let him get a ride back with one of his friends."

"Oh, I'm glad, Jordan," Millie said. "That boy's been working so hard, he deserves a reward."

"My thinking exactly," Jordan said. "I'll go and honk the Jaguar's horn. That ought to bring him back to the house."

He left, but was back within a few minutes, and Millie and Tiana had not heard the sound of a car horn. The two women looked toward Jordan curiously as he entered the kitchen, an angry frown making creases on either side of his mouth.

"The Jaguar's gone."

"But—that's impossible," Millie stammered, clearly not having put two and two together as yet. "The extra key's in the cabinet here." To prove her point, she opened the cabinet door and stared at the empty hook where the extra Jaguar key was kept. "Why—it's gone!"

"And Farrell with it," Jordan snapped.

Tiana's disappointment in her brother was acute. She'd been thinking how well he was handling missing the party, while all the time he'd been working out a plan to get there by less than honest means. Still, a part of her did not want to believe that Farrell would actually take Jordan's car without permission. "I don't understand," she said. "The garage is so close to the house. Why didn't we hear the motor?"

Jordan brushed this aside with an impatient sweep of one arm. "He probably didn't start it until he was well away from the house. There's enough slope to the drive that he could have taken it out of gear and let it roll halfway to the gate."

"What are you going to do?" Tiana murmured, made more and more uneasy by Jordan's angry expression.

He ran a hand across his face, a rather harried gesture. "I ought to call the police!"

Tiana and Millie exchanged worried glances, and Tiana scrambled to her feet. "Jordan, you can't do that. Farrell hasn't stolen your car."

He made a furious grumbling sound. "I'd like to know what you call it then." Restlessly, he walked to the kitchen window and looked out. "Damn that stubborn little pup! I thought he was taking this thing too calmly."

"He's just gone to that party, Jordan," Millie said, watching him with genuine concern. "He'll be back after a while—scared to death and sorry for what he's done."

"He'll be even sorrier when I get my hands on him," Jordan retorted, still staring out the window, a tautness in his body. Then, after a moment, he seemed to relax and glanced at Tiana. "I'm going back to work. Call me the minute he shows up."

Tiana nodded and when he had gone she said to Millie, "How could Farrell do something like this!"

"He's still a boy," Millie said reasonably. "This is just one of those crazy kid things boys do sometimes. I raised three of 'em, and I know. Once my oldest son fell off a second-story window ledge at the high school at midnight and broke his elbow. He was trying to walk all the way around the building, going from one window ledge to the next. When I asked him whatever possessed him to try such a foolish thing, you know what he said? Somebody dared him." Millie shook her head. "That's a kid for you."

"What do you think Jordan will do to Farrell?" Tiana asked.

"Probably just give him a good lecture and make him stay at home for a couple of weeks. He'll work out most of his anger at his easel before Farrell gets back."

Tiana hoped Millie was right. Farrell deserved to be punished, but Jordan had looked, a moment ago, as if he could have cheerfully strangled the boy. She went out on the deck to alternately sit and pace restlessly for the rest of the afternoon.

A few minutes before six, a phone call came for Jordan. He was still in his studio and Millie went to get him. Tiana had heard the phone ringing out on the deck and came inside as Jordan appeared in the living room and picked up the receiver. The conversation was clipped and brief.

When he hung up, he turned to Tiana. "That was the Tahlequah police. There's been an accident."

Tiana felt her heart plummeting and she caught hold of the arm of the couch for support. "Farrell . . . is he . . . ?"

"He's hurt," Jordan said, "but they don't think it's too serious. He's in the Tahlequah hospital." He glanced over at the housekeeper. "We'll have to use your car, Millie. It's the only one here that's operating."

"Take it and I'll wait here until you get back," Millie responded, an anxious look in her brown eyes. "It won't matter how late you are." She went out to the kitchen and got the keys from her purse, handing them to Jordan. "Just let me know, as soon as you can, what shape he's in."

"I'll call you," Jordan said and turned to Tiana. "Let's go."

In Millie's old Ford, Tiana asked, "What happened? Did the policeman say?"

"Apparently Farrell and one of his friends were having a chicken race on the old south highway. Farrell came to his senses at the last minute and swerved to avoid hitting the other car, but he cut too sharply and lost control. The car hit a concrete guard rail support."

"Was—was anybody else hurt?"

Jordan shook his head. "The police found beer cans in both cars, so I expect there will be repercussions." He stared grimly through the windshield as they turned onto the highway.

The silence grew heavy. Tiana stirred uneasily. "Did they say anything about your car?"

"It's pretty banged up."

Tiana lapsed into silence. There was nothing else to say. It seemed to take a long time to reach the hospital even though Jordan was pushing the speed limit all the way.

Farrell was in a room at the end of a long hall. Tiana pushed open the door and saw him lying in bed, one leg swathed in white and supported by pillows on both sides. Relief swept over her when Farrell looked toward the door and she saw recognition in his eyes.

"Hello, sis—Jordan," he said in a low voice.

Tiana rushed to the bedside. "Oh, Farrell, are you all right?" Jordan followed her into the room more slowly.

"I only got a broken leg," Farrell said, his eyes going to search out Jordan's hard face. "Right below the knee. They said it's too swollen to put a cast on today. It's packed in ice." His eyes clung to Jordan's face. "I'm sorry, Jordan," he said now with the ring of earnest sincerity in the words. "I know I shouldn't have taken your car."

"No, you shouldn't have," Jordan returned, "and you certainly shouldn't have used it for one of those damn fool races."

Farrell gulped, his eyes drifting away from Jordan's unrelenting look. "Oh . . . you know about that, too."

"And the beer," Jordan continued.

"I wasn't drunk," Farrell said. "I only had one beer. Honest."

"You'll have to tell that to the police," Jordan told him, no sympathy apparent in his voice.

"Your Jag," Farrell said with infinite sadness. "I guess I smashed it too. I don't remember very well—" His eyelids were lowering and Tiana realized that he must have been given a sedative.

"I haven't seen the car yet," Jordan said. "It's been towed in to a garage. I'm going to go by there when I leave here."

Farrell struggled to keep his eyes open. "W-will your insurance pay for the repairs?"

"It doesn't cover teenage drivers," Jordan said flatly.

Farrell's eyes were closed, but he dragged them open again. "I'll pay for it. You can take it out of my wages. That is, if you still want me to work for you. I can do some things, even in a cast."

Jordan put a hand on Farrell's shoulder, unbending a little for the first time. "We'll work it out."

"I'll never have anything to do with those races again," Farrell murmured sleepily. "You told me it was stupid, Jordan, and you were right. Can—can you forgive me?" His words were becoming slurred.

Jordan gave his shoulder a pat. "We'll talk about it later."

Farrell was asleep, his dark head fallen to one side on his pillow. Jordan touched Tiana's arm. "I'm going to see if the doctor is around—and call Millie."

She pulled a chair up beside Farrell's bed and waited for fifteen minutes for Jordan to return. When he did, he said he'd talked to the doctor and learned Farrell wouldn't be released until Sunday.

Leaving the hospital they found the garage where the Jaguar had been left. The right front fender was crumpled like an accordion, but other than that the car did not seem to be damaged. Learning that it would probably be two weeks before the car could be returned to him, Jordan rented a car from the garage owner and followed Tiana, in Millie's Ford, back to the house.

Alone on the drive, Tiana drew a heavy sigh of relief. Farrell had not been critically hurt, the Jaguar could be repaired and, most surprising of all, Jordan had not heaped recriminations upon Farrell's head as Tiana had expected him to do. Seeing Farrell injured and repentant had taken most of the heat out of his anger, not that he wouldn't expect Farrell to pay for the repairs. But that was as it should be. It was a cruel way to learn a lesson, but Farrell seemed to have faced up to the irresponsibility of what he had done.

Back at the house, after Millie had gone home, Tiana was struck, for the first time, with the knowledge that she and Jordan would be alone in the house all weekend. Almost as if he sensed her discomfort at the thought, Jordan suggested that they take Saturday off from the portrait and visit the Cherokee Cultural Center complex, Tsa-La-Gi, south of Tahlequah. Some of Jordan's paintings were on display in the Cherokee National Museum there and, in the evening, they could see the outdoor drama, *The Trail of Tears,* which was performed nightly from May to September in the amphitheater at Tsa-La-Gi.

Tiana agreed readily, forgetting for the moment that she had told Dale she would be too busy Saturday to go out with him. Later in her room, when this did occur to her, she could only hope that she and Jordan didn't run into Dale in their wanderings the next day.

8

There had been a tension in the air since Millie went home Friday evening, leaving Tiana and Jordan alone. Consequently, Tiana did not expect to rest well Friday night and, indeed, it was some time before she could fall asleep. Once she did, however, she slept deeply, lying on her stomach with one knee bent and arms extended, dropping into the deepest reaches of sleep like an exhausted child. Hours later, after the Saturday morning sun had risen, she began to dream—languorous, sensuous dreams in which she lay in Jordan's arms and revelled in the touch of his lips and hands. Then, from ouside the dream, the sound of a movement penetrated her returning consciousness.

Groaning in protest, she curled on her side, wanting to drift back into the lovely dream she was having in which Jordan had just swept her up into his arms and was carrying her toward the woods. It had felt so warm and wonderful in Jordan's arms. . . .

Then a sound like muffled footsteps intruded and, reluctantly, she opened her eyes on broad daylight and sunlight flooding in through the partially opened draperies covering the sliding glass doors. Outlined against the sunlight, Jordan stood, looking down at her. For a moment, while her vision adjusted itself, she stared at him without speaking, wondering how long he had been there watching her. From the lazy looseness of her dreaming state, Tiana felt her body begin to grow taut. Jordan's expression was enigmatic as she rolled over onto her back and pulled the sheet up over her shoulders, stretching her legs and torso as she did so.

"I thought I'd better wake you," he said.

Even with her eyes half-closed against the bright sunlight, she was aware of his dark gaze moving over the outline of her body beneath the sheet. The contrast of the bright light surrounding his dark head gave the illusion of a halo. Tiana suppressed an ironic smile at the incongruity of this thought. "Is it late?"

"Ten thirty." He thrust his hands deep into the pockets of the navy trousers he wore with a navy-and-white-striped knit shirt.

She blinked at him, hardly able to believe that she had slept for almost twelve hours. "You should have awakened me earlier."

"I tried," he said. "I knocked at your door twice, but there was no reply." His glance skipped across the room and rested on the drapery-shrouded window in the south wall. "I was beginning to think you were already up and had gone off somewhere. So I decided to come in and check."

"Gone off somewhere?" she asked lightly, curious as to what was going on behind his taut profile.

His gaze came back to her, his eyes narrowing. "I sensed last night that you didn't feel comfortable about being here alone with me. I thought you might have phoned someone to . . ." He halted, seemingly unwilling to finish voicing the thought.

She frowned. "Phoned someone?" She stared at him. "Oh, for heaven's sake, Jordan. Did you think I had slipped away in the middle of the night like some scatterbrained teenager?"

"That did occur to me." The words were clipped, hard-edged. "You're not a late sleeper ordinarily." He turned to look through the glass doors. "I found some breakfast rolls left from yesterday and put them in the oven to warm. Get dressed and we'll eat and go in to see Farrell." He walked to the door and stopped on the threshold. Without looking back, he said, "Oh, by the way, Dale Gregory phoned. He wants you to call him back."

"All right," she said, smiling at the reluctant way he had delivered the message.

He turned toward her again. "Will you cancel our plans for the day to go out with him?"

"Of course not."

He nodded curtly and went out, closing the door behind him. He'd never admit it, she thought as she put on a cool, sleeveless dress of yellow silk, but he was looking forward to taking her to Tsa-La-Gi. She slipped her feet into comfortable low-heeled sandals, put up her hair, applied a few dashes of makeup, and joined Jordan in the kitchen for rolls and coffee.

They drove to the hospital to find Farrell with his right leg in a newly applied cast. He was leafing through a magazine which he tossed aside when he saw them.

"I've been hoping you'd come to see me today," he greeted them eagerly. "A policeman was here earlier. They've decided to forget about the beer and let me off with a warning. Whew! That was a relief! But I want to know about the Jaguar. How bad is it, Jordan?"

Jordan was examining the new cast. "It'll be in the shop for a couple of weeks, but it could have been worse." He looked into Farrell's troubled face. "You're lucky to get out of this with only a broken leg, you know."

"I'm sorry about your car," Farrell declared stoutly.

"You already apologized yesterday," Jordan told him, a surprising tolerance in his expression.

"I meant it when I said I want to pay for the damage," Farrell persisted.

"All right," Jordan returned.

Farrell relaxed against his pillow. "That's only fair." He rolled his eyes in an expression of disgust. "I can't believe I was that stupid." He turned to look at Tiana. "What's in the bag?"

She placed a brown paper bag on the table beside his bed. "Pajamas, underwear, a toothbrush, and a few other things."

Her brother grinned at her. "Thanks. Especially for the pajamas. I hope I can get them on over this cast. I hate these hospital gowns. It's embarrassing."

Both Tiana and Jordan laughed and, after a moment, Farrell joined them. They stayed for a half hour. As they were leaving, Jordan said, "We'll be here to pick you up after lunch tomorrow."

"Don't be late," Farrell called to them as they started down the hall.

Tiana looked up at Jordan. "Thanks for not giving Farrell a lot of I-told-you-so's."

He shrugged. "I think Farrell is heaping enough recriminations on his own head without my help."

"You're not much for holding grudges, are you?"

This time his glance was lingering and there was a sardonic lift of his lips. "You say that as if it surprises you."

She shook her head. "No. I do think it's a nice trait to have."

"Ah, ha." They had reached the hospital entrance and Jordan swung open the door so that Tiana could pass through before him. Outside, as they walked toward the rented car, he continued. "You're beginning to see a few saving graces in my otherwise black character. Who knows, you might even get to like me."

"I like you already," she said truthfully. "I'd like anyone who was such a good friend of my grandfather's."

"I see," he retorted with a rueful look. "I guess that puts me in my place—in case I might be getting any ideas. Right?"

"Right," she answered lightly.

The short drive to Tsa-La-Gi was made in silence; but it was a comfortable sort of silence, Tiana thought gratefully. They parked in a graveled area and walked toward the museum building. Tiana had been there several times, and she could still feel a swell of pride at the sight of the Cherokee National Museum which housed the greatest collection of material written by or about Cherokees to be found in any one place in the world. The building was modern in design, faced with sandstone native to the area, and surrounded by a reflecting pool which extended into the lobby. In front of the wide glass entrance the three remaining columns from the old Cherokee Female Seminary, which was built in 1851 and had burned in 1887, had been left as a solemn reminder of the tribe's early achievements in the Indian Territory.

The Jordan Ridge Exhibit was on display on the second level.

"Most of these will be shipped to Paris in August," Jordan told her.

Tiana soon lost herself in a leisurely study of the paintings, wandering slowly from one to another, heedless of other museum visitors or anything else that was going on around her. Jordan ambled off to look through some new additions to the museum archives. He returned to the gallery almost two hours later to find Tiana standing before one of his recent works entitled simply "The Old Ones," a painting of five elderly Cherokee men sitting around a campfire on an autumn night, passing around a pipe and reminiscing.

She glanced at him as he came to her side. "This one," she said, pointing to a face seen in profile, half lost in shadow. "It's Grandfather, isn't it?"

"I wondered if you would notice," he told her. "I had him in mind as a model when I painted it, although it's done from memory. Do you like it?"

"Oh, yes," she breathed. "It's the most beautiful painting I've ever seen. I—I would like to own it some day."

"You couldn't afford it," he said curtly, causing her to look at him sharply. He wore a closed expression and she said no more about the painting, surmising that it was one he did not want to part with. In his own way, he had been very fond of her grandfather.

"Are you ready to go?" he asked. People were beginning

125

to recognize Jordan and a few were watching them curiously. Clearly, he did not find the celebrity role a comfortable one.

"Yes," Tiana said. "Do we have time to walk through the village?"

He glanced at his watch. "Sure, if you'd like. It's only four."

The Living Village, another part of the cultural complex, was only a short walk from the museum. There, Indians portrayed the daily life of a Cherokee village of the 1700s for the benefit of groups of visitors led by Cherokee guides. Tiana and Jordan joined a group that was leaving the entrance as they arrived. Both had toured the village on several previous occasions; nevertheless, they found themselves intrigued again by dancers with tortoiseshell rattles strapped to their legs, women weaving mats and making pottery, and boys playing stickball.

When the tour was finished, Jordan took Tiana's arm and they walked back to the car. "I'm starved. I just realized we didn't have lunch."

"We had a very late breakfast," Tiana reminded him.

"Well, now it's time for an early dinner—a long, leisurely one—and I know just the place. Have you visited that steak house north of Tahlequah?"

"No. I've passed by it several times and wondered how the food was. But I've never been inside."

"We'll go there then," Jordan decided without consulting her further. The Cherokee painter could certainly not be said to be indecisive, she thought with secret amusement.

The steak house proved to be a homey combination of red tablecloths and knotty pine paneling with country-western tunes playing softly in the background.

"Nothing fancy," Jordan said when they were seated at a small table next to the wall, "but the cook knows how to broil a steak."

They ordered filets which, happily, lived up to Jordan's promise and, afterward, lingered over sherbet and several cups of coffee. Tiana was feeling quite sated and relaxed until a high-pitched voice pierced the gentle murmur of diners' conversations.

"Why, Jordan!"

Startled out of her somnolent reverie, Tiana looked up to see Lois Graham in hiphugging slacks and a tight knit shirt, standing beside their table.

"I've been trying to call you all day."

Jordan, seemingly as surprised as Tiana to see Lois there, got slowly to his feet. "Hello, Lois."

"Gracious, honey, where have you been?" Tiana had the distinct feeling that Lois was studiously avoiding acknowledging her presence.

"To the museum and the village," Jordan told her as Tiana tried to read something in his expression, but failed. "We've been away from the house most of the day."

"We?" At last the sharp blue eyes swung around to regard Tiana. "Oh, hello there, Tiana. So you're the one who took my fella off where I couldn't find him?"

Tiana felt herself flushing. After an embarrassed silence, she said, "Would you like to sit down, Lois?"

She caught the slight shake of Jordan's head too late, but Lois said, "I can't. I'm here with a friend." She glanced briefly over her shoulder where a man Tiana had seen around town was standing just inside the entrance, watching them.

"He owns the building where I have my dress shop," Lois explained with a coy glance at Jordan. "We're negotiating a new lease." The blue eyes slid back to rest on Tiana's face. "Still living with Jordan, Tiana?"

Flustered, Tiana started to reply, but Jordan cut her off. "Both Farrell and Tiana are staying at my place for the summer, Lois. I told you that before."

"Dear me . . ." Lois fluttered thick eyelashes at him. "Yes, you did, honey, but I never really believed Tiana would stay that long. Being a teacher and all. I mean . . . Not that I pay any attention to gossip myself."

"I'm glad to hear you say that, Lois," Jordan snapped, his displeasure obvious in the tight line of his lips.

Lois looked at him for a moment, as if she weren't sure what to do next. Then she gave a brittle little laugh. "I'd better get back to my business meeting. Call me soon, Jordan, you hear? Good-bye now." Without looking at Tiana again, she sauntered across the dining room to the table her escort had taken.

"Let's get out of here," Jordan grumbled, tossing the tip on the table.

Tiana followed him to the cash register and then out to the car, avoiding a glance toward Lois's table, although she sensed that Lois's eyes never left her and Jordan. Never had Tiana witnessed such naked jealousy in anyone's manner and words as had been in Lois Graham's.

Jordan turned the car north and drove through the wooded countryside surrounding the town. After a long, strained silence, Tiana said, "Lois thinks we're . . ." She halted in embarrassment.

"She knows," he said harshly. "She knows I'm attracted to you—that I want you."

Staring resolutely at the dusty, sun-dappled road, she said finally, "But she believes that we're . . ."

Jordan's hands tightened on the wheel. "Naturally, she thinks we're lovers. If Lois were in your place, that would be a foregone conclusion."

"I don't like people thinking that," Tiana said deliberately, "even though you don't seem to be bothered by it."

The car surged forward, taking a corner at reckless speed, then gradually slowed again. "You're right," he said with a sideways glance at Tiana, who was sitting stiffly beside him. "I don't give a damn what people think. I'm sorry that you do."

She studied him in silence for a thoughtful moment. "You really don't understand why I'm concerned about it, do you?"

"No," he said flatly. She waited for him to go on, but he did not.

Her thoughts wandered to another puzzling aspect of the man beside her. "What about Lois? You must have some feeling for her. You've been involved with her for a very long time."

"Depends on what you mean by involved," he said tensely. "But I don't intend to discuss Lois with you."

Recognizing the stubbornness in the thrust of his jaw, she said quietly, "Sorry."

After a moment, he seemed to relax against the seat. "No, I'm sorry. I didn't mean to bark at you. Let's just forget about Lois—and everybody else and enjoy the evening." He astonished her then by reaching for her hand which lay on the seat between them and clasping it warmly in his own. They drove in silence and, after a while, Tiana's eyes were drawn to their clasped hands. She felt detached from them. It was an odd feeling and she continued to sit quietly, as if to move or speak would break the spell of contentment that seemed to have descended on them.

It had grown dark by the time they reached the amphitheater at Tsa-La-Gi, although it was still fifteen minutes before the drama was scheduled to begin. Jordan found a parking place and, releasing his grip on Tiana's hand, switched off the motor and pocketed the keys. They got out without speaking.

A narrow path through a wooden park led to the amphitheater. Walking beside her, his hands thrust into his trouser pockets, Jordan asked suddenly, "Did you return Dale Gregory's phone call?"

"Yes. Before we left the house this morning."

"Did you tell him you were spending the day with me?"

"No," she said shortly.

She sensed impatience in the tautness of his lean body. "Well, what did you tell him?"

"I don't know what business that is of yours," she said stiffly, sadly aware that the contentment she had felt in the car had dissipated and the tension that was becoming all too familiar between them had replaced it. Feeling him tighten up even more, she relented a little. "I merely said that I had already made other plans."

He laughed. "He accepted that?"

They had stopped walking and were facing each other. She felt disappointed at what seemed to her his deliberate disgruntlement. What had she done to make him start picking on her like this? "I've told you before, Dale trusts me. Of course he accepted my explanation."

"I wouldn't!" With a sigh that seemed compounded of despair and defeat, he reached out for her, pulling her slowly toward him, so close to him, she could see his eyes brooding over her face. "Dale Gregory is a fool to let you get away from him." He sounded driven and the bleakness in his eyes disarmed her. This was a new Jordan, one who seemed bedeviled, even unsure, and she did not know how to rebuff him.

His mouth came down slowly to wander tentatively over her face, searching out the vulnerable places—eyelids, cheeks, the corners of her trembling mouth. Hardly aware of what she was doing, she turned her lips to his. Then, like magnets that could not resist each other's drawing power, their mouths came together hungrily. His lips moved yearningly over hers, and she felt the blood racing through her veins like liquid fire, as if every nerve end in her body was raw, exposed to his touch. She returned the kiss searchingly, softening and melting into him.

With a softly muffled moan, he released her lips to gaze down at her, eyes narrowed.

"Jordan," she murmured dazedly, her lips still a-tingle with his kiss. She wanted more of his kisses. She wanted his arms about her, his hands caressing her. Never had she felt such a flood of longing engulf her, filling her with desire. . . .

As if he could see all of this in her eyes, his arms tightened around her and he began kissing her again, his lips leaving hers after a long exploration, to search out the tender spot beneath her earlobe and trail warmly down her neck to kiss the hollow at the base of her throat. His hands traced the outline of her narrow waist and the ripe young breasts which strained against the confining silk of her dress and pushed against his titillating hands. For long moments Tiana was lost in the rising tide of her flooding emotions. She never wanted him to stop touching her, kissing her. Her hands ran over the hard muscles of his back, loving the feel of his body under her fingertips.

He crushed her even closer, pressing his cheek against her hair. His breath came raggedly and she heard the rapid thunder of his heart. "Oh, God, Tiana . . ." he said thickly. "How long are you going to deny me what we both want so desperately?"

What we both want . . . The words echoed through the churning chambers of her mind and, slowly, she began to get a grasp on her runaway senses. Yes, she wanted him to make love to her—more than she had ever wanted anything in her life. That would be enough for him, but she knew that she wanted, had to have more. Foolishly, recklessly, she had allowed him to invade her heart—but she had not touched his. He desired her body, yes—and she would be an even worse fool to go into a relationship like that. Eventually it would destroy her. She stepped back.

"What's wrong now?" The words came through his clenched teeth.

"Nothing . . ." she said shakily. "I—I can't do this."

"For the love of God, Tiana!" There was a dangerous edge to the tone. "Do you *enjoy* shoving me back and forth like a yo-yo? Is that how you get your kicks?"

"No . . ." Wounded, she shook her head. "I don't mean to do that. I'm sorry."

"Sorry!" That one explosive word sounded so harsh and unrelenting. "We seem to say that to each other a lot."

She drew in a deep, steadying breath. "Jordan," she said quietly, "you want to own me, but you don't want to give anything in return. Oh, I don't know . . ." She ran an unsteady hand across her eyes. "Maybe you can't help it. Maybe you've already given the important parts of yourself to your work. Maybe artists have to do that."

"Spare me the psychoanalysis," he said bitterly.

She didn't know what else to say to him. "If we don't

hurry, we'll miss the beginning of the show." She started walking toward the amphitheater and he fell into step beside her.

"We certainly wouldn't want that to happen, would we?" he jeered. "I'm sure you prefer vicarious experiences to real ones. So much less disturbing."

She could not match his sarcasm and did not even try. They found their seats in the amphitheater just as the lights dimmed and the performance began. Somehow Tiana managed to push what had happened in the park out of her mind and lose herself in the dramatic events being acted out on the stage below.

The play began in the winter of 1838 along the Trail of Tears with Cherokee Chief John Ross grieving for his wife who had died from the hardships of the long march. It traced the Cherokees' courageous efforts to establish a new home in the wild Indian Territory, explored the differences between the eastern and western elements of the tribe, followed the long efforts of Chief Ross to unite the nation only to have his efforts thwarted by the Civil War which, once more, saw the two factions on opposing sides. The final scenes of the drama portrayed the long period of rebuilding following the war and the gradual bowing to the inevitable loss of their nation as, in 1907, the Indian Territory became a part of the new state of Oklahoma.

During the performance Tiana had almost forgotten that there were nearly 2,000 other people in the audience; she was hardly even aware of Jordan sitting beside her. It was something of a jolt to come back to reality when the lights came back on and people began to stir and talk. She looked over to Jordan, who was getting to his feet, and smiled tentatively. "I'd like to bring Farrell to see this when he's out of his cast. He saw it several years ago, but now I think he might be able to appreciate it more. I want him to know our history."

"Yes, maybe we can bring him later in the summer." The tone was matter-of-fact and, as they began moving with the departing crowd toward the exit, Tiana felt relieved that Jordan no longer seemed angry with her. In spite of their differences, she sensed a bond between them—the bond of their mutual heritage. Perhaps Jordan sensed it, too, for on the drive home he talked easily enough about trivial things.

Encouraged by the friendly mood, Tiana took the opportunity to say, "I know I've been too critical of your handling of Farrell. These past few weeks have made me see that discipline is what he needs."

He looked at her with a wry lift of an eyebrow. "What brought this on?"

She shrugged. "I realized at the hospital yesterday—and this morning, too—how much Farrell respects you. He was so earnest about getting back in your good graces and wanting to pay for the damage to your car. Your good opinion is very important to him."

"I'd like to think that Asudi would approve."

"He would," Tiana said with certainty. "Grandfather knew exactly what he was doing when he named you Farrell's guardian."

A faintly mocking smile flickered on his lips. "You didn't think so at the time!"

"I admit it," she replied, "but it's a woman's prerogative to change her mind."

"So I've noticed," he retorted.

They had reached the house and, when they were inside, Jordan turned on the lights in the living room. Then he surprised her by saying, "Have a glass of wine with me."

She had intended going straight to her room, but to refuse his request seemed rude. "That sounds nice," she said. "I'll get the glasses."

When she returned, Jordan had taken a bottle of wine from a cabinet in the dining room and was sitting on the couch. He filled the two glasses and lifted his to her in a silent salute that made her wonder what he was thinking.

She sipped her wine, her dark lashes sweeping down over her eyes. When she looked back at him, he was

133

watching her. She swallowed. "It seems so strange here without Farrell. . . ."

His mouth hard, Jordan said, "Perhaps I should have left you in a motel, but it's twenty-five miles back to town and very late."

She should have known his amiable mood wouldn't last. "I didn't mean . . ."

He surveyed her unsmilingly. "I know exactly what you meant, Tiana. All your suspicions are well known to me."

She felt the blood leave her face, and she stared at him with angry eyes. "You're enjoying this, aren't you?" she accused. "You kept me out here deliberately by asking me to have a glass of wine so that you could insult me. You know I'm trapped here."

Jordan's face grew still and hard, as if it were chiseled from brown stone. He set his wineglass down on the coffee table and faced Tiana with a stillness that frightened her. "I suppose I encouraged Farrell to take my car and run it into that bridge so that I could get you alone." His eyes were blazing with fury now. "Believe me, after that little scene in the park tonight, I don't relish being alone here with you." The frosty eyes that raked over her rigidly angry body were contemptuous. "You're safe with me, Tiana. I have no inclination to touch you. I don't find the thought at all appealing."

"Oh, really!" she flung at him, hurt by his words and remembering his passion in the park. "I suppose you didn't like kissing me and—mauling me tonight."

A muscle beside his mouth twitched with suppressed tension. "I liked it about as well as you did."

She set her wineglass beside his on the coffee table. "Having wine together wasn't such a good idea, was it?" she said with bitter resignation. She stood, then added hesitantly, "Regardless of what you think of me, I did enjoy the day. Thank you." He merely looked up at her without reply, and she turned to move toward her bedroom. After a few steps, she paused, then faced him again. "Jordan, I wish—"

He turned his head to look at her, anger still there in every taut line of him. "Don't suggest again that we be just friends! I think things have gone a little too far for that to be possible, don't you?" He drained his glass and got abruptly to his feet.

"I don't know," she said wearily.

He merely grunted at this and stalked toward his bedroom, banging the door shut behind him. She heard his muffled footsteps on the carpeted floor, then an almost unearthly silence settled over the house, bringing with it a feeling of desperate loneliness. Tiana sighed deeply and walked slowly through the living room, turning out the lights. Then she felt her way through the darkness to her bedroom.

9

"Hold still, can't you!"

It was Sunday morning and Jordan had asked her at breakfast if she would pose for an hour or two. Searching his face for a sign that he was going to continue the verbal thrusts with which he had assailed her the night before, Tiana had reluctantly agreed. The session was not going well, however. For some reason, Tiana was in such a state of nervous tension that she felt almost as if she could jump out of her skin.

"I—I'm sorry, but I have to rest my neck a minute."

He laid his brush aside and, leaning back in his chair, peered from behind the easel at her with waiting eyes. She sat straight on the chaise longue, rubbing the back of her neck with one hand, then stretched the cramped muscles of her arms. From beneath lowered lashes, she stole a glance at Jordan. He had been so silently withdrawn all morning that she had no way of guessing what he was thinking. From time to time, as now, his dark eyes had looked like deep pools, calm on the surface but underneath a sort of churning, almost tormented, look.

Ah! she sighed internally, chiding herself for being so fanciful. Jordan was feeling nothing but impatience at her inability to hold a pose this morning. She settled back into her half-reclining position on the chaise. "I'm ready now."

He got up and moved her arm back into position; then, running his hand beneath her hair, he let his fingers rest warmly on her nape. Tiana looked into his face, wondering if this was a deliberate provocation. She had the most ridiculous desire to press back against his hand, to feel his strong fingers caressing her neck. Their glances met and she saw that deep stirring in the brown depths of his eyes—or imagined that she did.

Yes, she must have imagined it, for he muttered an impatient growl and lifted her long hair so that it fell forward across her left shoulder and arm like a black silk fan.

"Hold that pose," he said curtly and returned to his easel. For the next half hour, she managed to stay in that position, even though every muscle in her body seemed to be screaming for relief. Why, she wondered, was it so much more difficult to sit still today?

Jordan worked with a frown of intensity on his face, glancing at her occasionally, but she could not discern anything personal in the look now. She might as well have been another piece of furniture, she concluded crossly, and then wondered why this thought should irritate her to such an extent. He had said himself that she was doing him a great favor by posing for him, and yet as the sessions had come and gone he had seemed more and more irritable or, what was somehow worse, so absorbed in paint and brushes that he forgot she was there.

Her left arm, which took part of her weight, had gone to sleep. She sighed distractedly and worked her fingers in an effort to get the blood circulating again.

"What is wrong with you today?" Jordan held his brush in mid-air and scowled at her.

She sat up, abandoning her effort to hold the pose. "I'm tired. Can't we stop now? I have to fix lunch."

He gazed at her for a long moment, then put his brush down. "Go on then. You're no good to me jumping around like a worm on a hot lid."

His unflattering description caused hot anger to rise in her. She flounced to her feet. "Too bad I'm not a—a robot that you can program to behave exactly as you wish!"

"Yes," he muttered darkly, "that *would* be an improvement."

She stopped at the door, hands on hips, glaring; but he

had already turned away to clean some brushes, as if her reaction were of no interest to him. She pressed her lips together and left the studio.

After changing from the white tunic to jeans and a cotton blouse, she went to the kitchen to take a meatloaf and potatoes from the oven and a strawberry salad from the refrigerator. When the table was set, she called Jordan and he came promptly, turning all of his attention to eating the meal she had prepared as if he were starving. Tiana, who had been ready to defend herself against further insults, felt perversely let down.

After lunch they drove to the hospital to pick up Farrell, who was waiting for them with great eagerness. He'd managed to pull on knit slacks over his cast and showed off his ability to handle his newly acquired crutches by setting off down the hall at a brisk clip.

Back at the house, Tiana thought it would be a relief to have a third party around again. She helped Farrell up the steps of the front porch.

Farrell made it clear that he had not had a decent meal since he left, and so she settled him at the kitchen table and served him what remained of lunch.

Satisfied that Farrell was managing nicely, Jordan excused himself to go to his room.

When he had finished eating, Farrell insisted on going outside for a reunion with Duke, and then he practiced using his crutches by traversing the deck several times. Finally, tired from his exertions, he returned to the living room and stretched out on the couch.

Tiana was changing channels on the television set, searching for the sports program Farrell wanted to watch, when Jordan came into the living room, having changed into dove-gray trousers and a burgundy silk shirt.

"I'm going out for a while," he announced.

"Shoot!" Farrell exclaimed with genuine disappointment. "I was hoping we could play backgammon this afternoon. You promised you'd teach me—and it's going to get awful boring around here with this cast slowing me down."

"I shouldn't be late," Jordan said. "If you're still awake when I return, we can have a game."

"Well—" said Farrell ungraciously. "If you *have* to go."

"I'll play with you, Farrell," Tiana said.

"I guess I'm not in the mood, after all," Farrell replied as Jordan left.

He's going to see Lois Graham, Tiana told herself. Remembering his crossness with her all morning, resentment spread its heavy fingers through her body. Shortly he will be with a woman who appreciates his company, she thought bitterly.

She found the sports program and, although she had little interest in it herself, she sat down in a chair near the couch to be near Farrell in case he needed anything.

"I wonder where Jordan was going all dressed up," Farrell said, still clearly miffed that his guardian would desert him his first day home from the hospital.

"I have no idea," Tiana replied shortly.

Farrell twisted his head around to look at her. "You mad at him or something?"

"Of course not. Why would you think that?"

He was still looking at her. "You been acting kind of funny ever since you came to the hospital to get me. You and Jordan both—like you'd had an argument or something."

"I'm preoccupied," she said, "wondering how much it will cost to get my car running again. As for Jordan, you ought to know by now that he's moody and not particularly thoughtful of other people's feelings."

"Gosh, why do you say that?" Farrell's eyes widened in surprise. "I think he's being a real sport about the Jag. Even if he is making me pay for the repairs. He could have raked me over the coals good and proper, but he hasn't been half bad about it."

"I admit," Tiana said grudgingly, "that he's been fair about the car. Just count yourself lucky that you weren't here when he first found out that you had taken it. He might have strangled you."

"I can't much blame him for being upset," said Farrell with amazing objectivity. "That car's a beauty—and I did take it without asking. I was mad because I wasn't getting to go to the party, but that was really a dumb thing to do."

Tiana regarded him with a slight smile, gratified at the note of maturity in the words. "I'm glad you realize that."

He laid his head back down on the arm of the couch. "You know, sis, being around Jordan has made me think about some things."

"Such as?"

"All the hard work I've been doing around here—it's made me realize I don't want to have to do that kind of stuff all my life. Not for a living, I mean. I want to find something I like so much I can do it all day and enjoy it so much I lose track of time—like Jordan and his painting. I've been thinking about going to college in the fall."

Tiana found that she was speechless for a moment. Was this really her brother talking, the boy who had scorned studying in high school, the boy who had declared he couldn't wait to be done with teachers and books and school?

"Why, I think that's wonderful," she said finally.

"Do you?" He grinned sheepishly. "I know it'll be expensive, but Jordan said he'd help me with that if I keep my grades up."

So Jordan had been talking to him about going to college. That's where this had come from. "I don't think that will be necessary. The rent from the farm should be enough to cover room and board and tuition, provided you go to a state school."

"Do you think I can handle the science courses in prevet?" he asked, worry clouding his face.

Tiana's surprise grew with each new sentence her brother uttered. "I think," she assured him, "that you're bright enough if you are willing to work hard."

"That's what Jordan said," he told her seriously. "He said I've got a way with animals."

"You've certainly given this some thought."

He shrugged. "A guy's gotta plan for the future. Jordan said nobody's going to hand you anything on a silver platter. You gotta work for it."

Jordan said . . . Jordan said . . . Tiana stifled an impulse to remark cuttingly about Farrell's guardian. After all, her brother was saying things she had longed to hear. He was showing signs of growing up, a development she had fervently hoped for. Apparently, Jordan deserved much of the credit for the amazing transformation.

"Jordan's right, of course," she replied, hoping that Farrell could not detect the reluctance with which she made the admission.

They watched television until seven when, at Farrell's request, she made hamburgers and french fried potatoes for their dinner. They ate in the living room from TV trays. Then she cleaned up the kitchen while Farrell went out to the deck to sit with Duke for a while. As Tiana wrapped the remaining uncooked ground beef and returned it to the refrigerator, she imagined Jordan and Lois Graham having an intimate dinner in Lois's apartment, certain their menu would include something more sophisticated than hamburgers.

About eight, Farrell came back into the house, looking weary. "You'd better go to bed now," Tiana told him. "You shouldn't overdo your first night home."

"Yeah," he agreed readily. "The doctor said I ought to take it easy for a day to two."

He went to his bedroom and got into his pajamas. When Tiana came in a few minutes later, he was already in bed. "Take your sleeping pill," she said, offering him the pill and a glass of water. "The doctor said you should have one for two or three nights so your leg won't keep you awake."

When he had swallowed the pill, she propped his leg on a pillow and tucked the sheet around his waist. "Call if you need anything," she said as she turned out the light.

" 'Night," he murmured sleepily, his eyes already drooping.

142

Alone again, the restlessness that she had experienced earlier in the day returned. Tiana tried to watch television, but could not get interested in the available fare. She flipped off the set and wandered through the house, finally going out to the deck to lean against the railing and stare into a summer darkness that was filled with the sounds of crickets and frogs and, from somewhere to her right, the lonely hoot of an owl.

She hadn't been on the deck long when a wind began to rise and move through the trees with a melancholy soughing. The wind picked up quickly, tossing twigs and leaves onto the deck, sending Duke to the shelter of the garage and Tiana indoors.

By that time daggers of lightning could be seen in the south and, as Tiana moved through the rooms, closing the few windows that were open, a loud clap of thunder shook the house. It began to rain then, large pelting drops at first and finally slanting sheets of water that swished against the windows.

Tiana went to check on Farrell, fearing that the storm might awaken him, but he was dead to the world. The sleeping pill had done its work.

She wondered briefly if Jordan was out in this, on the road from Tahlequah perhaps, but she pushed the worry aside. She had no doubt that Jordan was quite capable of taking care of himself. Still restless, she finally took a bath and dressed in nightgown and robe, returning to the kitchen to make tea. There would be no sleep for her as long as the storm continued.

As she was pouring the boiling water over the tea bags in the pot, thunder ripped through the sky and the lights went out. Tiana stood at the kitchen cabinet in the blackness and experienced the beginning of fear.

Now, don't be silly, she scolded herself. There were candles in the cabinet—she had seen them several times—and matches on the range. She felt along the cabinet doors overhead, and, finding what seemed to be the right door, she swung it open and ran her hand over the dishes on the shelf until she touched the side wall. But the candles weren't where she remembered seeing them.

Stifling her growing trepidation, she opened the next door. Then she heard something that made her jump. Above the pelting of the rain against the windows, there was a scratching that sounded as if it came from near the back door. This was followed by a piercing howl.

Duke! It was the collie trying to get in, frightened from his shelter in the garage by the thunder. Feeling along the wall for the rack, Tiana's fingers fell on a towel and she grabbed it, turning to make her way as quickly as she could to the back door in the utility room which adjoined the kitchen.

When she opened the door, rain hit her in the face and a dripping Duke pushed his way past her legs. She shut the door quickly, then bent to the shivering collie, who was cowering beside her, and began to rub his fur with the towel and murmur comforting words. Duke was properly grateful for being allowed inside and insisted on reaching up to lick her face, which was bent over him. Tiana stepped away, repulsed by the odor of wet dog. The towel was wet through, anyway.

"Stay," she commanded the dog, as she had heard Jordan do.

Although she could not see Duke, she heard him settling himself on the tile floor. He was evidently more than willing to oblige her, perhaps fearing to be put outside again if he didn't.

At that moment, a deep male voice made her start with fresh fright. "What's going on here? Tiana?"

It was Jordan. Duke got to his feet eagerly, his claws scrabbling against the slick tile, and Tiana turned to him again with the command to stay. The dog lay back down, whining in protest.

Tiana started back toward the kitchen, feeling her way. "I'm in the kitchen, Jordan," she called.

She heard a muttered curse as he evidently ran into

something. "Why are you walking around in the dark?" he demanded, the sound of his voice nearer this time.

She had found the kitchen door and stepped across the threshold, feeling for the cabinets. "The electricity is off. Do you think I *like* stumbling around in the dark?"

A chair leg scraped against the floor as he ran into it. "Where are the candles?"

"I couldn't find them."

He began to open doors at the other end of the cabinet and, after a moment, he said, "Here they are. Hand me a match."

She fumbled for the box on the range, took out several matches and made her way to Jordan's side in the dark. The hand which took the matches from her was cold. Then a small flame flared and came down to light the candlewick.

He set the candle on the kitchen table, lighted another, and left it on the cabinet. Then he turned to Tiana, his eyes restlessly moving down her body.

"Were you afraid?"

"Not really, only put out because I couldn't find the candles." She glanced down at her thin pink nylon robe and flushed hotly, realizing how the soft material clung to her body. "I—I was about to have a cup of hot tea when the lights went out. Would you like one, too?"

He nodded, his look raking the bare cabinet top and range. "I don't suppose there's anything left from dinner."

"There's hamburger meat, but no way to cook it with the electricity off. I thought you'd . . ." She halted, puzzled. If he had taken Lois out, surely they'd had dinner. The imagined intimate scene in Lois's apartment came back to her mind and she felt confused. Maybe he hadn't seen Lois after all.

He was looking at her with a vague expression. "You thought what?"

"N-nothing," she stammered. "I could fix you a ham sandwich. Does that sound all right?"

"Anything would sound all right. I'm starved." He sat

145

down at the table and ran both hands over his damp hair, pushing the disheveled strands away from his face.

She went to the refrigerator and took out the sandwich material, feeling his eyes on her as she carried it to the cabinet and prepared the sandwich, then two cups of tea.

Tiana set the food on the table, then sat down across from Jordan. Although she had turned off the air conditioning earlier, the kitchen felt slightly chilly. Cold rain blew against the windows. Tiana wrapped her fingers around her warm cup and sipped the tea slowly, enjoying the heat rising from the cup to warm her face. Jordan ate his sandwich in silence. The sound of the storm outside made the kitchen seem cozy, in spite of the drop in temperature.

When the sandwich was finished, Jordan leaned back in his chair and gazed at her. "Farrell doing all right?"

"Yes," she said quickly—too quickly, perhaps, for she was glad to be able to talk and dispel the amtosphere of strangeness in the kitchen. "He stayed out on the deck for a while, and when I said he should be in bed he agreed without an argument. I gave him a sleeping pill, so I don't expect he will stir until morning."

"Good. We'll ask Millie to keep an eye on him tomorrow, make sure he doesn't overexert himself."

Tiana nodded absently and got up to pour herself another cup of tea. "Want more?"

He shook his head and she returned to her chair. She leaned forward, elbows on the table, cup held in front of her. "How long do you think the storm will last?"

"Not long, I would guess." There was a tightness in his tone.

She looked over the rim of her cup at him. His eyes were on her body where her flimsy robe gaped open in front, exposing the pink lace of her gown. The burgundy shirt, still damp, clung to him like a second skin, giving him a magnificence that made her heart quicken.

"Aren't you chilled in those damp clothes?" she asked to divert his attention.

"No," he said, and his eyes lifted to her face. "You're very fetching in that get-up."

She managed a smile, flushing. "Thank you."

"Don't be coy, Tiana," he said tightly. "You know you're beautiful."

"No, I—" She paused. "It's nice to be told I am, at any rate," she finished softly.

Another loud roar of thunder broke into the charged atmosphere. Starting, Tiana set her cup down and got to her feet, pulling her robe more tightly about her. Restless, she moved to stand at the window over the sink and looked out at the stormy blackness.

"The storm *is* making you uneasy," he said accusingly.

Still watching the rivulets of water coursing down the windowpane, she admitted, "A little. I can never sleep during a storm. When I was a child, I used to hide under the covers when it thundered."

She heard Jordan's chair scraping as he got to his feet but did not look around. Momentarily, he moved to stand behind her, his hands on her shoulders. "That doesn't sound like a Cherokee girl to me."

She saw the hazy outlines of their reflection in the window glass, Jordan's dark head above her own, and did not move.

"Don't you remember Asudi's tales of how Thunder befriended the Cherokees?"

"Vaguely," she said, made to feel suddenly shy by his nearness and the hands resting on her shoulders.

Then his fingers moved down her arms. "You're shivering," he said and wrapped his arms around her body, pulling her back against him, surrounding her with a delicious warmth. She let her head fall back to rest against his broad shoulder, remembering the times Asudi had come to her during a storm to hold her and comfort her.

"Wasn't there a story about the monster Uk'ten' and Thunder?" she murmured, wanting to keep him talking, wanting to remain in the warm security of his arms.

"Yes." His lips moved gently against her hair.

"Tell me," she said, her eyes half closed in contentment.

"There are several versions," he said, "but the one I like best is the one about the two boys who were out hunting when they heard several loud blasts. They followed the sound into a valley and saw a huge, horned dragon—Uk'ten', of course—wrestling with Thunder. As they fought, Thunder's blasts became weaker and weaker because the monster had enveloped Thunder in his coils. Thunder called to the boys to help him, promising to be their friend for life. Uk'ten' said Thunder was lying, that he would kill the boys if he got free.

"Eventually, the boys decided to believe Thunder and shot the monster with their arrows. He was only wounded, though, so they had to run for their lives. Thunder told them to build seven fires on their way home because only fire could finish off Uk'ten'. The boys did as Thunder said, barely keeping ahead of the monster, who survived the first six fires, growing weaker all the time with Thunder roaring at him as he lumbered along. But the seventh fire was too much for Uk'ten' and he died."

Jordan paused, and his arms settled themselves more comfortably about her, just below her breasts. "Then Thunder told the boys, 'You can always depend upon me. While we live on earth we must protect and help each other.'"

These were the exact words she had heard Asudi say many times, and then her grandfather always finished the story with another comforting statement of Thunder's. Automatically, Tiana murmured the final words of the story as Jordan fell silent. "And Thunder said, 'Do not be afraid. I am the ruler of all the fierce things in the world.'"

They stood motionless for several moments until slowly Tiana became aware of the pressure of his arms against her breasts and the deep, strong beating of his heart. She realized that the hands at the ends of the crossed arms were cupped warmly along the sides of her breasts and she felt, with a rush of her senses, the muscles of his chest hard

148

against her back, his muscular thighs solid against the soft roundness of her hips.

Her eyes, which had been dropping with warm drowsiness, flew open, and she turned to look up at him, a strange dizziness sweeping over her. She stood, helplessly waiting, her body clamoring for more of his touch. He bent his head very slowly and she could not move away.

His hard, cool mouth touched her lips and a shudder of responsive heat ran through her. His hands came up to catch her shoulders and pull her against his body, holding her, while his mouth did its tantalizing work, warming, softening, opening her lips, leaving her blind and helpless. Under the hot, fierce exploration of his mouth, she was unable to think, clinging to him, kissing him back, while his hands pressed her closer and closer.

Outside, the rain continued, splattering against the windows, shutting them into a small, warm, private world, as the long sensuous kiss continued. Then, abruptly, he wrenched his mouth from hers. Blinking, dazed, she looked into his face.

The dark brooding eyes were tortured. He let her go suddenly, the brown depths leaping with tormented feeling, his jaw tense as though he were suffering acute pain. She looked back at him, feeling her senses calming, her awareness of things outside herself returning, as if she were waking from a dream.

He breathed harshly. "All right." The words were ragged. "You win, Tiana. I'll marry you."

For a few brief seconds, joy pierced her heart, but, too soon, reason asserted itself, and she knew what he was offering was not what she wanted. Striving for a calm tone, she said, "Jordan, you don't mean that."

"I wouldn't have said it if I didn't mean it," he returned, his voice hard. "You've made me see that there are a few things in life a man has to have or lose his grip on his sanity—even when the price is far too high."

Price! The word hammered home even more assuredly

what she had known all along. His proposal was nothing more than a trade-off, a business proposition. "My body is not for sale," she said, but there was no anger in the tone, only resignation.

He laughed bitterly. "Everything is for sale, Tiana, if the price is right."

Tiredly, she murmured, "Jordan, let's forget these last few minutes ever happened. You can't really mean to marry me just to get me into bed."

"Dammit, I do mean to!" he exploded. "Other men do it all the time. Few marry for any other reason. I have to have you, Tiana. It's that simple. I'll do anything to get you."

"Even walk unprotesting into my clever female trap?" she inquired wryly.

He looked at her furiously, eyes burning. Then a groan escaped him. "Yes," he admitted. "You've subdued me, Tiana. You've won. I'm willing to do this your way now."

"You don't understand me at all," she said, shaking her head. "I don't want to marry you on your terms."

"*Your* terms," he said through clenched teeth.

She shook her head again. "No. I can't imagine anything worse than living with a man who would always feel he'd been trapped into marriage. We would end up tearing each other apart." She managed a shaky smile. "You'll thank me in the morning when you're calm enough to realize that you still have your precious freedom."

"Freedom!" he jeered scornfully. "How can I be free when the mere sight of you sets me on fire?"

"Then I'll go, Jordan," she said flatly. "I didn't think I could move out and leave Farrell behind, but I see now that there is nothing else to do."

His nostrils flared. She met his incredulous gaze without flinching. But even while she was calm on the surface, inside she ached with love for him, burned with a desire that prompted her to go back into his arms and let him do whatever he wanted with her.

"You will not move out!" he said harshly.

"I have to," she said quietly, drawing on weeks of pretending indifference to him, although it was agony to see that tortured look on his face.

His mouth curved in an ugly sneer. Without warning he grabbed her and held her rigidly still in his strong hands. "You will stay here until I finish the portrait. The least you can do is keep your word on that." His eyes blazed into hers. "Promise me you will stay. Say it, Tiana."

"All right," she whispered, afraid to oppose him further. "I'll stay until you've finished the portrait."

He continued to stare down at her for a moment, then let her go and turned away stiffly to lean against the cabinet. "Get out of my sight." The savage hardness of the words stunned her. She walked out of the kitchen on unsteady legs.

In the darkness, Tiana guided herself along the hallway wall until she found the steps that led to the lowest level. Still trailing her hand on the wall, she descended and found her way to her bedroom.

Throwing off her robe, she crawled into bed, pulling the sheet and bedspread over her. She drew herself into a knot and lay shivering, while long-dammed tears spilled down her face. Pain was becoming a familiar companion. Why did love have to bring such anguish?

The temptation to marry Jordan, on any terms, had been so great, and the struggle to deny him so difficult, that she now felt drained of strength.

Still, a part of her regretted her decision. Even a marriage on Jordan's coldly calculating terms would have given her something. She loved him and she wanted him desperately. But, after their passion had been satisfied, what of those calm moments of reflection? In those moments—and they were sure to come—she knew the unhappiness over being married to a man who did not love her would overwhelm her.

10

Tiana had not expected to run into Dale during Monday's lunchtime crush in the off-campus restaurant. She had hoped to be able to eat her salad in solitary reflection, while she tried to make some sense of the jumbled state of her emotions.

He had seen her, however, and was coming toward her with a smile on his lips, a rather stiff smile, she noticed absently, as she made herself greet him in a tone that rang—if falsely—with enthusiasm.

"I didn't expect to see you here today," she said. "I was prepared to eat my lonely lunch and wander over to the university library for a while."

He wore a lightweight tan suit and there was a tiny streak of blue ink on one cheek; he had obviously just come from his office. He sat down at her table and now she saw the tension lines on either side of his mouth. He had not been smiling at all, but grimacing.

"You look all wrung out after your busy weekend." The sarcasm in his voice was so unlike Dale that Tiana could only stare blankly for a moment.

"Well, yes, it was rather busy. I brought Farrell home from the hospital, and—"

"Home!" He cut her off scathingly. "So now Ridge's place is home!"

She frowned. "That isn't what I meant to convey, Dale, and you know it."

"*Do* I?" His hazel eyes narrowed, and he leaned forward to say, with harsh emphasis, "I don't know anything about you anymore, Tiana. I look at you and I see a stranger."

"Dale, what . . . ?"

But she could not finish, for at that moment a young waitress arrived to take Dale's order. He told her curtly to bring him coffee and a cheeseburger without ever taking his eyes off Tiana's face. The waitress, with whom Dale customarily joked and passed pleasantries, glanced at Tiana with a raised eyebrow and left.

"Are you getting a kick out of having two men pursue you? Is that it?" His fingers dragged his napkin off the table and thrust it into his lap in an angry gesture.

Tiana, who had thought she would manage during lunch to put things in reasonably proper perspective, felt her cheeks grow hot with another surge of unwanted emotion. "What's come over you? I can hardly answer these sarcastic questions of yours unless I know what has made you so angry."

"The questions are rhetorical, Tiana," he snapped, his fingers gripping the handle of the knife beside his plate. "I already know the answers. I had an extremely enlightening talk with Lois Graham this morning."

"Lois? What are you doing talking to Lois? I thought you said you hardly knew the woman."

"She telephoned me at the office," he said tightly, "and stop trying to turn the tables and put me on the defensive, because it won't work. I want to know what you think you're up to."

"More loaded accusations," she responded indignantly, "but I'm afraid your meaning escapes me. Forgive me if I'm slow on the uptake today. You will have to spell it out for me."

"After giving me the runaround, you spent Saturday— all day and, for all I know, all night—with Jordan Ridge. Lois saw you together."

"So that's it! Lois saw Jordan and me having dinner and jumped to her dirty little conclusions. From what I know of her, that's about par, but I resent her spreading these vicious rumors all over town!"

"You needn't play the innocent victim," he hissed at her, the words straining between unmoving lips. "Ridge told Lois you'd been out at the cultural center together earlier in the day and she saw you that night at the amphitheater."

"Lois was there!" Tiana fumed. "Why, that conniving female followed us!"

"She didn't follow you," he denied. "She was there with a man—her landlord, I think she said. She also said the two of you were so absorbed in each other at dinner that she had to walk right up to your table or you'd never have seen her."

"That is a bare-faced lie!"

The waitress brought Dale's cheeseburger, her glance going from Tiana's angry face to Dale's angrier one. She set the plate down without a word and hurried away.

"Tell me," Dale went on in that same low, deliberate voice, "is he a good lover?"

"You have no right to insult me like this," Tiana flared. "Jordan is not my lover. I resent this, Dale. You owe me an apology."

She hoped that her words rang with conviction, but she was all too aware that the spirit, if not the letter, of her bald assertion was less than true.

"I'll apologize, Tiana," he said tensely, "when I'm convinced there is something to apologize for." He grasped his knife and cut his cheeseburger in half with an angry, slicing motion. Picking up one half he looked back at her with furious hazel eyes. "Farrell was in the hospital all weekend, so you were out there alone with Ridge. That must have been cozy!"

"I can't believe you would take that woman's word over mine!" Tiana blinked back hot tears of indignation.

"You have given me no evidence to the contrary," he said stubbornly.

"Evidence!" The word was shrill. "What is this, an inquisition?"

"Why would Lois Graham call me, a virtual stranger, and lie?" he persisted doggedly.

155

"Because she's consumed by jealousy. She thought she could get Jordan to marry her, and now she's beginning to see that isn't going to happen. She is striking out at me because—because I'm there."

He bit into the cheeseburger and chewed slowly. Then he sipped his coffee and said, "If Lois Graham is all wrong about you and Ridge, why did you tell me you had other plans for Saturday and then spend all day and evening with him?"

For a moment, she was silenced. Then she said haltingly, "It was all very innocent, Dale. He—he has some paintings on exhibit at the Cherokee museum that I wanted to see. My grandfather was in one of them—and, well, after that, we had to eat—and—"

"You had to go to the amphitheater, too, I suppose, just to finish off a totally innocent evening."

Tiana sighed and sagged in her chair. "I don't know why I'm even trying to explain. You are determined not to believe me." She was on the point of excusing herself and leaving Dale to finish his lunch alone when she looked up to see Nancy Pearson approaching their table.

"Hi, you two," the redhead caroled. "Mind if I join you? There aren't any available tables at the moment." Her hand on the back of an empty chair, she looked from Dale to Tiana inquiringly.

"Sit down, Nancy," Tiana said, embracing the diversion provided by her friend's cheerful presence.

Dale was finishing his cheeseburger quickly, ignoring Nancy altogether. As the redhead sat down, he swiped at his mouth with his napkin and got to his feet. "I have to leave now." He glanced at Tiana, a frosty, stubborn look on his face. "We'll finish our discussion later." Then he strode away.

Nancy grinned impishly at her friend. "Not very subtle, is he? Apparently I interrupted something."

"Thank heavens you did," sighed Tiana. "We were having a dreadful argument."

"So," murmured Nancy, wrinkling her faintly freckled nose. "All is not billing and cooing with the lovebirds." She turned to the harried young waitress who was passing at that moment. "Jilly, just bring me a chef's salad and iced tea." Turning back to Tiana, she continued, "Aren't you going to eat your lunch?"

Tiana picked at a lettuce leaf disconsolately. "I'm not hungry. I'm still too upset by the awful things he said to me." She glanced at her friend, her dark eyes rekindling. "Do you know he had the nerve to accuse me of having an affair with Jordan?"

"Any truth to the accusation?" inquired Nancy mischievously.

"No! I mean, we haven't been to bed . . ." For some reason, Nancy's direct green gaze made Tiana feel uncomfortable.

"But?" Nancy's eyes widened. "Do I detect an unsaid but at the end of that statement?"

"Of course not!" Tiana exclaimed. "The thing is Jordan and I are together a lot—we would have to be, living in the same house—and then, of course, he is painting my portrait. Dale insists on making too much of everything."

"He's painting your portrait? How interesting." Nancy tossed tumbled red waves away from her face. "Naturally, Dale is jealous. What do you expect?"

Tiana darted an impatient glance at her friend. "You know he has no reason to be."

"Do I?" said Nancy lightly. Without waiting for Tiana to respond, she went on breathlessly, "Has he kissed you?"

It was sometimes difficult to follow Nancy's abrupt shifts in conversation. "Who, Dale?"

Nancy cocked her head to one side and gave Tiana a knowing look. "Come on, kiddo. You know I don't mean Dale. Has the sexy Cherokee painter kissed you?"

"Well, uh . . ."

"He has!" Nancy pounced. "When? How did it happen? Come on, Tiana, curiosity is killing me."

"Actually, it has happened more than once, but—"

"More than once!" The green eyes glowed with avid interest. "Twice?"

Tiana's hand went up to smooth her chignon. "Stop cross-examining me, Nancy. I didn't keep track."

Nancy clapped her hands in delight. "Gracious, Tiana, the look on your face is a study. You are certainly having an exciting summer out there in the country, aren't you? Oh, I'm so envious I can't stand it!"

"Well, you needn't be," Tiana returned dampeningly. "I—I've never been so confused and—and unhappy in my life."

The words carried such conviction that Nancy became immediately solicitous. "Tiana, I'm sorry for teasing you. Oh, don't tell me, yes, it's true, isn't it? You're in love with the man!"

There was no point in denying it. Nancy knew her too well. So Tiana nodded mutely.

"But that's wonderful! Why are you looking so downcast about it?"

Tiana drew a deep breath. "Because it's Jordan. Because I've fallen in love with a man who loves no one. Where women are concerned, he—he's an animal. His heart, his soul are in his work."

Nancy's look was incredulous. "An animal, huh? Wow, I'd like to pursue that—but I can see it would do me no good. Now, you listen to me, Tiana. When the time and the woman are right, any man can fall in love."

Tiana's wave of one hand was a gesture of weariness. "I know you believe that, Nancy. But Jordan is not like other men."

"Nonsense! All men are alike in that way."

"You don't know him as well as I do."

"Well, of course, that's true," Nancy said, dimpling with mischief again.

Tiana tried to smile. "I may be moving into town before the summer's over, after all. If your invitation is still open, that is."

158

"Of course it's still open. I'd love to have you share my apartment. But surely you aren't thinking of giving up Jordan Ridge without a fight."

"I can't give up what I never had," Tiana retorted.

Nancy studied her in silence for a moment. "Whenever you want to move, just say the word."

As the remaining hot July days passed, Tiana managed to avoid another confrontation with Dale, even though he phoned her several times. She continued to sit for the portrait. Except for those long, mostly silent but wearingly taut sessions, she and Jordan avoided each other as much as possible. She knew that her refusal to marry him had wounded his enormous pride. Tiana wished that she could make him understand how she felt—but that was not possible unless she was willing to humble herself and admit that she was hopelessly in love with him.

On several occasions, in fact, when they were alone in the studio, she almost blurted out everything. One day, after she had finished posing, she left the chaise longue and went to one of the huge windows to look out. South and east of the house, the land rose gently in tiered hills across which were scattered blackjack oaks, hackberries, elms, and cedars. With the sun lowering, the wooded hills were darkened by long shadows. They looked secluded and secret and Tiana could almost imagine the mythical Little People of the Cherokees coming out of their secret places to cavort in the small hidden valleys.

Standing there with the late afternoon sun slanting through a corner of the south window, bathing her in its golden glow, she stretched slowly, feeling her nakedness beneath the thin white tunic and luxuriating in the warmth of the sun.

Suddenly, Jordan, whom she thought was cleaning his brushes, came up behind her and, lifting her long hair, began to massage the back of her neck and the tight muscles in her shoulders.

"You were a good model today," he murmured, his

strong fingers sending delightful relaxation all through her body. "This portrait is probably the best thing I've ever done. Another week or so and it'll be finished."

"Then you'll let me see it?" she inquired lazily, letting her head drop forward as his fingers continued kneading.

"Uh-huh," he murmured softly.

"Oh," she sighed with pleasure, "that feels wonderful . . ."

"Uh-huh," he said again, and his hands worked their way lower, along her rib cage, sliding gently across her breasts, cupping the ripe fullness and pulling her back against him. He buried his face in her hair, whispering, "Ummm. You smell so clean and feminine. . . ."

They stood like that for several moments. She closed her eyes, feeling the warmth of the sun, the sweet torment caused by the slow sensual movement of his hands. She had almost told him then, almost blurted out, Jordan, I love you! At that moment she had come so close. . . .

But the knowledge that, however much he desired her, he did not feel the same thing for her as she felt for him had stayed her tongue. Refusing to acknowledge her love was the one scrap of pride she had left, and she was determined to hang on to it.

She did not want to pull away. She wanted to give in to the slow seduction of his touch and her own burning passions. But she did not—could not. She moved, breaking his gentle hold, and said, "Millie will be needing my help in the kitchen."

One swift glance at him took in a hard mouth and tortured eyes. She knew that she could soften that mouth, could wipe away the torture in the eyes—but it would cost too much in terms of heartache and shattered emotions. Inevitably, the price would be extracted from the depths of her very being. So she left him.

Nothing like those few tender moments had passed between them again, and soon July gave way to August and Tiana's classes at the university came to an end.

She posed for Jordan every morning during the first week of August, wanting the portrait to be finished as devoutly as he appeared to want it. He seemed driven now and worked in the studio for at least ten hours each day. Tiana did not know what he did after noon, when she no longer posed, but assumed he was perfecting the portrait. Or perhaps working on other things.

On Friday of the first week in August, Millie took Farrell into town to see the doctor so that Jordan and Tiana could continue with the portrait. It was only a checkup for Farrell; it would be another ten days before the cast would come off.

In the studio, Jordan's face was set in harsh lines as he worked. Since that afternoon when he had held Tiana, she had been aware of the increasing strain between them. Would he never finish the portrait? she wondered bleakly, as she reclined on the chaise longue. She didn't know how much more of this enforced nearness to him she could survive. It was becoming harder and harder to meet his look, to talk about the weather or Farrell. Her love for him held her so tightly that she sometimes felt as if she were smothering, and she believed that the only way she would ever begin to be free of him would be to leave his house.

Farrell had enrolled at Oklahoma State, more than a hundred miles away, and would be moving to Stillwater at the end of August. Tiana had almost decided not to wait until Farrell was gone to move in with Nancy. She had to get away from Jordan, and as soon as the portrait was finished she would be able to go. She began to plan a plausible explanation of why she was moving out before Farrell left for college.

Suddenly, Jordan tossed his brush aside and shoved his chair back. "That's it."

Tiana sat up on the chaise. "You mean it's finished?"

He nodded, running both hands across his tired features and through his thick black hair.

"Let me see!" she exclaimed, eager anticipation taking her over.

"No." He raised a hand when she started to stand. "Sit right there. That's about the right distance for the best

161

viewing." Slowly, he stood and, reaching out, turned the easel around to face her.

Then he stepped back, and she stared at the portrait. Her likeness half-reclined on the canvas, black hair tumbling over one shoulder in lovely disarray. The suggestion of the outline of one breast seemed to push against the white tunic. The lips were soft, parted very slightly, and the dark eyes looked out at Tiana as if they knew a wonderful secret. It was Tiana Vann, all right—but somehow so much more.

For a moment, she felt as if the breath had been squeezed from her lungs. "It—it's lovely—" she faltered.

Jordan, who had been watching her reaction closely, nodded. "As you are."

Tiana shook her head, her long hair falling about her. "Oh, no, Jordan, it's too much—too beautiful."

He came to stand in front of her, looking down. He said quietly, "It's how I see you."

She looked into his face, saw the moistness which stood out on his forehead and around his mouth.

"You like it, then?"

Her eyes clung to the beloved contours of his face and she nodded. "Oh, yes—oh, Jordan—" Dear heaven, she was going to cry!

The drawn features relaxed as he sat down beside her, smiling in an indulgent sort of way. He took her into his arms and his lips moved against her hair, his breath warm. "Why are you crying?"

With her tearful face pressed into the moist skin of his neck, she could think of nothing but the heaven of being in his arms again. It seemed years—ages—since he had held her, and now she was where she wanted to be.

"I—I don't know," she whispered, her voice breaking a little on the words.

He had been wanting this closeness, this touching too. His trembling flesh told her that, and the moist heat of his body spoke of the anguish he had been suffering. His hand at her nape, his fingers moved almost involuntarily among the thick tresses. She sensed that he was making a valiant effort to control himself, but the thunderous throbbing of his heart would not be hidden so easily.

Tiana clung to his strength with an urgency born of the torments she herself had been suffering for weeks, uncaring of the pain in her heart caused by the knowledge that he did not love her. The waiting, the fierce yearning had wracked her for too long. . . .

Her whole body surrendered to the closeness of his embrace, and she had no thought of tomorrow, or even the next minute, no thought for anything but herself and Jordan. She loved him; she *needed* him. . . .

As if her feelings were being communicated to him, Jordan drew away a little, looking down at her with eyes full of passion and something else that she could not understand. "How much of this do you think I can take?"

This time it was Tiana who could not stop. "Please, Jordan, kiss me—"

His features contorted and his arms tightened around her once more. His breath was expelled in a tortured groan.

"Oh, Tiana!" he muttered in a strange voice, and then he was kissing her desperately, his mouth devouring her with hot sweetness. When, after long honey-sweet moments, he released her mouth, she protested with a little sigh, but he did not mean to let her go.

"Tiana," he murmured, emotion thickening his tones. "Oh, Tiana, you're in my blood. I've tried to get you out, but I can't. Do you have any idea what it's been like these past weeks, seeing you, being near you and not being able to hold you like this?" His lips could not resist touching the contours of her face, returning again and again to the moist eagerness of her mouth.

For several minutes, Tiana could not reply. With Jordan covering her face with kisses, she could think of nothing but him and the hardness of his body that the tight-fitting

163

jeans did little to disguise. His shirt was open in front, and her fingers spread themselves over his unyielding bronze chest with sensuous delight.

"Jordan . . ." His name was her very breath.

He lifted her head slightly and she met his dark eyes, catching her breath at what she saw in them. "You cannot resist me any more than I can resist you, my beautiful Tiana," he muttered, unfastening the buttons of her tunic with fingers that shook a little. "Neither of us is free." He bent his head to her breast. "Will you deny that, Tiana?"

While his tongue stroked the hardening tip of her breast, his hands threaded themselves through her hair and caressed the sensitive skin of her neck and shoulders.

"No, I won't deny it," she murmured weakly.

His mouth returned to hers, his tongue gently outlining her lips until she was so hungry for him she had to wind her arms around his neck and press his head down, forcing his mouth hard against hers.

After long moments, he growled huskily, "Don't keep this up unless you are prepared to take the consequences."

Tiana blinked, trying hard to think coherently, while his eyes searched her face unsmilingly. Her hands moved slowly over his back beneath the shirt, loving the feel of him.

"In another moment," he said unevenly, "I won't be able to stop."

But it was already too late. She was too dizzy with pleasure and longing to want him to stop, even if he could. She tilted her chin and kissed his lips slowly, deliberately.

"Tiana . . . ?" His lips moved against hers, and the way he said her name—the one word filled with desire and pleading—twisted in her heart.

She could not deny him—or herself. "Yes. Oh, yes, Jordan . . ."

He pushed the tunic off her shoulders, his eyes black and smoldering. "My sweet, beautiful Tiana . . . please, don't hate me—" He bent his head to explore her body with his lips.

164

"How could I hate you," she murmured, her lips moving against his hair, tasting its texture and cleanliness, "when I love you so desperately?"

She felt him go still for an instant and then he looked into her eyes—surprise and confusion warring with the overflowing passion. But the passion won, and with a deep sigh he claimed her mouth again, as if he could never get enough of her.

The only sound in the studio was their labored breathing, until, into the silence, someone called.

"Jordan! Tiana! Where are you? We're home!"

Farrell's words were filled with impatience, and the sound of his crutches clumping along the hall toward the studio sounded ominously loud in the silence.

Gasping, snatching for her tunic, Tiana's whirling senses reordered themselves with a rude jolt. Watching her, Jordan's face hardened and he got to his feet and moved toward the door.

"We're in the studio, Farrell."

As Tiana's shaking fingers refastened the buttons of her tunic, she heard Jordan fling open the studio door.

"Gosh, how long are you going to work?" Farrell inquired baldly.

"We're just finished," Jordan said, and Tiana wondered how Farrell could fail to notice the heavy irony in his tone.

She got to her feet, her legs trembling.

Manuevering his crutches, Farrell clomped into the studio. "The doctor said my leg's doing great. Man, will I be glad to get rid of this cast. Hey, sis, where are you going?"

"To the kitchen," she said as she brushed past Jordan and her brother and, without looking at either of them, left the studio.

When she was at the top of the stairs that led to the middle level of the house, out of sight of both the studio and the kitchen, she stopped and, gripping the banister with one hand, tried to compose herself.

Oh, God, what had she done? She had told Jordan that she loved him. She had offered herself to him, held nothing back. He had been deeply affected by their lovemaking, had wanted her with a blazing desire. She had seen all of that in his eyes. Yet he had not said that he loved her. No matter how much he wanted her, he would not say what he did not feel.

With trembling fingers, she smoothed her tangled hair, then started down the stairs. Her thoughts darted about in her head like mice in a cage but, in the end, there was only one way out. She had to leave this house, which had become a torture chamber, had to leave without delay.

11

After changing her clothes and putting up her hair, Tiana found Millie in the kitchen peeling potatoes.

"Let me do that," Tiana said.

Millie started to dismiss the offer of help, as she often did, but she hesitated, perhaps seeing in Tiana's face a need to be busy, and handed her the paring knife.

The housekeeper moved about the kitchen, preparing other dishes for the evening meal. For several minutes, Tiana stared at the long, curling pieces of brown potato peel her knife was creating. Then she cleared her throat. "Millie, you remember I told you about my friend Nancy Pearson's invitation to share her apartment? I—I've decided to accept. I will probably be moving out in a day or two."

She could feel Millie's eyes resting on her back and turned to look at the short, plump housekeeper, whose face contained an expression of perplexity.

"Farrell won't be leaving for college for another two weeks," Millie said. "I didn't think you'd want to be separated from him until you had to. What's the big hurry?"

"The new term will be starting for me soon, too," Tiana told her, striving for a lightness in tone that she was far from feeling in fact. "I thought it would be nice to be all settled in before the first day of school." For some reason, she was having trouble meeting Millie's searching, curious gaze, and she turned back to her potato peeling.

"Have you told Farrell you're moving?"

"Not yet," Tiana admitted. "I'll have to do it tonight, I suppose. You—you will look after him, won't you, Millie?"

The older woman made a disgruntled sound. "You know you don't even have to ask that question." When Tiana did not speak, Millie went on. "Do you mean to stand there and tell me this all-fired hurry of yours is due simply to wanting to get settled before school starts?"

"Why, yes." Tiana glanced over her shoulder.

Judging by Millie's ironic expression, she did not believe this. The housekeeper gave a tight little laugh. "I wasn't born yesterday, Tiana. You and Jordan have been shut up in that studio for days now. Knowing Jordan, I suspect he's gotten a bit too familiar—and that's why you feel called upon to leave so sudden like."

"Don't blame Jordan." Tiana laid down the paring knife and turned to face Millie. "He wouldn't force himself upon a woman. It's just . . ." Her voice trailed away uncertainly.

Millie looked at her with widening eyes, her face full of sudden speculation. "Just that you're in love with the big, stubborn lout?"

Tiana smiled nervously. "You're a hopeless matchmaker, Millie—especially where Jordan is concerned. But you're barking up the wrong tree this time."

The older woman's dark eyes ran over Tiana in quizzical surmise. "Meaning that you *don't* love him?"

"Meaning," said Tiana carefully, "that Jordan is not the sort of man a girl falls in love with—not if she's smart."

Millie surveyed her thoughtfully, a slight frown creasing her forehead. She bent over the range, stirring the contents of one of the stainless steel pots. "I never noticed," she said pungently, "that being smart has very much to do with falling in love." She replaced the lid on the pot and turned to look at Tiana again. "I don't know what's happened between you two, but something's been wrong with Jordan for weeks now. He walks around with his mind off somewhere else. Half the time, if you say anything to him, he bites your head off."

"His mood will probably improve when I'm gone,"

Tiana said half apologetically. "He finished the portrait today, so there is nothing to hold me here any longer."

Millie's eyebrows rose steeply. She looked at Tiana with a light slowly dawning in her eyes. "So you admit his black mood has something to do with you? To tell the truth, Tiana, I have thought once or twice that he might have asked you to marry him. Has he?"

Nervously, Tiana said, "Yes, but it was only in a weak moment. I think he regretted it the minute the words left his mouth."

"Pshaw! What a childish notion!" exclaimed Millie. Her voice had a firm ring to it. "Jordan is the last man in the world to suggest something like that on the spur of the moment." She shook her head. "Rest assured, he gave it careful thought before he spoke, and he meant it."

Remembering his disappearance during the hours before that odd proposal, when she had believed him to be with Lois, Tiana suspected now that he might have been driving alone, thinking. "Well, it doesn't matter," Tiana told her. "I can't marry him."

Millie's indignant look was almost comical. "Can't marry him! I never heard such twaddle in my life! The two of you are made for each other!"

"You don't understand, Millie," said Tiana sadly. "Jordan doesn't love me. I couldn't live with a man under those circumstances."

"My dear girl." Millie's tongue clicked against her teeth. "If you expect him to kneel at your feet or shower you with flowers or some other such tomfoolery that you might have read about in a book, you're far off the mark. Jordan's an odd mixture. He's proud and stubborn and mighty independent, but he's also easily hurt." She regarded Tiana seriously. "Don't you love him?"

Tiana's throat felt dry. She swallowed and said softly, "If I did, that would be even more reason not to marry him. It wouldn't work."

Millie looked at her with a penetrating stare. "I know

Jordan about as well as I know my own sons. I can feel it when something is stuck in his craw. I've had that feeling whenever I see the two of you together. I can't say for certain, of course, but I'd swear that Jordan has never asked a woman to marry him before. Surely that means something."

Moistening her lips, Tiana said, "Maybe, but it's not enough."

Millie smiled wryly. "You think I'm being a nosy old woman?"

"No!" Tiana spoke with certainty. "I know you want to help, but—" She shrugged. After a pause, she said huskily, "Okay, I'll admit that I love him. But he doesn't love me, and that's the whole story in a nutshell." She felt her face flushing at the humiliating admission.

Millie looked at her gently. Lowering her eyes, she said, "He's tried to get you in bed, I suppose."

Tiana made a low, shamed sound of surprise.

"Oh, my dear innocent girl. I know Jordan is no angel. I've heard the tales about him and all those other women. Not that I believe everything I hear, mind you. If Jordan had done all they tell about him he would never have had time to set foot in his studio—but I'm sure there have been some women in his life."

Tiana glanced about the room, finding it too difficult to meet Millie's concerned look. "I haven't been to bed with him, Millie."

"I suspected as much," said Millie softly. "The way he's been snapping and brooding around here. A satisfied man doesn't go on that way for days on end."

Tiana shrugged helplessly. "Now you understand why I have to leave. I'll move in with my friend in Tahlequah, and I probably won't see him again. I'll make arrangements for Farrell to visit me at my place before he leaves for school."

Millie sighed with disappointment. "Don't you think you could stay a while longer—give it a little more time?"

Tiana shook her head, blinking back the hot moisture

that lately seemed always to be near to brimming in her eyes. "I've got to get away from him."

"I'll speak plainly, Tiana, and after I've had my say I won't try to change your mind again. I think you are making a terrible mistake. It's my opinion that you should marry him. Jordan is unhappy—anyone with one eye can see that. Marriage to the right woman is what he needs."

Tiana looked aghast. "You ask too much of me, Millie."

"He needs you," Millie said regretfully. "I've never known him to be this affected by any other woman. Do you really think you couldn't be happy as his wife?"

Tiana pressed trembling hands to her face. "Don't keep on at me, Millie, please."

The shrill ringing of the telephone intruded, and Farrell's voice came from the living room. "Tiana! Dale Gregory wants to talk to you."

Millie looked at her intently. Tiana called back, "Coming, Farrell."

In the living room, she took several deep breaths before speaking into the receiver. "Hello, Dale."

"I want to see you tonight," he said bluntly. "We have to talk."

Suddenly another confrontation with Dale seemed preferable to staying in the house with Jordan scowling silently and Millie casting her pleading glances.

"All right," she said. "I can be ready at seven."

"Fine. I'll see you then. Watch for my car. I'd prefer not coming in." He rang off without another word.

All during the dinner with Dale, Tiana had worked valiantly at keeping the conversation turned away from personal matters. Now, however, Dale had stopped his car on the grassy shoulder alongside the graveled road, only a few feet from Jordan's silver-colored mailbox, and she knew he would not be put off any longer.

He turned toward her in the dim, shadowy interior of the car. "I'll take you on up to the house after we've come to an understanding."

"All right, Dale," she said flatly, too tired to practice evasion any longer.

She could feel his eyes going over her and could just make out his grim expression. "I won't be given the runaround any longer, Tiana." His voice was tight with angry feelings. "Do you realize what a fool you've made me look? I'll bet Ridge has been having a good laugh at my expense! I asked you to marry me and you put me off, saying you needed time to think it over, and then you spent the summer out here with *him*. My God, I never believed you were the sort of woman who toys with men's emotions—as if they were puppets on strings. You've behaved shamefully, Tiana. I'm not at all sure I can forgive you."

"Listen, Dale," she said, her voice sounding bitter and tired. "Why can't you understand that I have stayed at Jordan's this long only to be with Farrell?"

"Do you honestly expect me to believe there has been nothing between you and Ridge—not in all this time? How big a fool do you think I am? The gossip is true, isn't it?"

"I'm not his mistress!" Tiana said despairingly.

"Tiana," he said, his tone drawling unpleasantly, "There is only one way you can convince me of that."

She sank back against the car seat, dropping her face into her hands. "What way?"

"Move out of Ridge's house right away and marry me as soon as we can get the license." There was no softness in the words, only a hard challenge.

But it didn't matter. She knew now that she could not marry Dale. She couldn't marry anyone, feeling as she did about Jordan.

She raised her head. "I've already made plans to move out of Jordan's house," she said quietly, "but I can't marry you, Dale. I'm sorry."

His fist came down on the steering wheel, making a resounding smack that startled Tiana, causing her to jump violently.

"Then you've been lying to me all along—about you and Ridge! I may have been a stupid fool, Tiana, but you're an even bigger one! As soon as he gets tired of you, he'll drop you like all the others!"

"I can't make you believe that there is nothing between Jordan and me," she said sadly, "so I see no reason to talk about it any more. I—I'll get out here and walk to the house." She fumbled for the door handle and, feeling it cool and hard in her hand, opened the door.

"Don't come running back to me when he throws you out!" Dale snarled, and Tiana didn't think she had ever heard such spite in anyone's voice before.

She stepped out of the car and, slamming the door behind her, walked briskly up the drive toward the house, not looking back.

Behind her, she heard the motor accelerating and tires skidding on gravel as the car roared away into the darkness.

Tiana realized that her whole body was trembling. She slowed her pace, drawing out the walk to the house. Pushing stray wisps of hair out of her face, she tried to find some ray of light in the gloom of her life. But she found none.

The summer had been a disaster. She'd fallen in love with a man who scorned love. She'd turned down two marriage proposals because to accept either would have made her life even more unhappy than it already was. Farrell was moving to another town, dependent on Jordan instead of his sister for whatever guidance he might yet need. And now she didn't even have Dale's undemanding company to fall back on. He had become as demanding and cruel as any other man.

It appeared that there was only one course of action open to her. She would bury herself in her work and she would survive, the same way she had survived the broken engagement two years ago.

Edward Shipman, she thought bitterly, a sob catching in her throat. Two years ago she had thought no one could ever mean as much to her as he, and now she couldn't even bring his face to mind. She wondered if she would recognize him if she should ever meet him again and thought it quite possible that she wouldn't.

The face that haunted her every waking minute now, causing more pain that she had ever known in her life, was the unyielding brown face of Jordan Ridge.

Back at the house, she found the living room deserted and took the opportunity to phone Nancy and pave the way for moving in with her friend the next day. As it happened she did not, however, have a chance to tell Farrell of her plans to move into town until the next morning, when she called him into her bedroom where she was already packing.

It was clear that her brother did not understand why she was determined to move that very day. "I don't get it, sis," he kept saying. "It's only two weeks until I start college. Why can't you wait until then to move?"

She had tried to give him logical reasons—her desire to be settled before her new stint of teaching duties started, Nancy's desire to have Tiana move in with her as soon as possible, the feeling that she had imposed upon Jordan's hospitality long enough, the fact that with the portrait finished there was nothing to prevent her going.

In the end, after Farrell's repeated urgings to change her mind, she had turned to him impatiently and said, "I have to go, Farrell, so please don't keep badgering me to stay. Believe me, this is best for everybody." Then, impulsively, she had thrown her arms around her brother's neck and hugged him.

Obviously, this rather enigmatic assertion which seemed at odds with her actions did not clarify things for Farrell, for he looked even more puzzled. But he did stop pleading with her to stay and promised to get Millie to take him to town to visit Tiana before he left for college.

It was Jordan whom she dreaded facing, however. As if he sensed her feelings, he had stayed out of sight since the embarrassing debacle in his studio the previous afternoon. She assumed he was in the studio now, for she caught no sight of him as she carried her things outside and loaded

174

them into her car. She assumed, also, that he knew what she was doing and had opted to make it as easy for her as possible by keeping out of sight until she was gone. This assumption, though, proved to be quite wrong.

She was loading the last of the boxes into the trunk of her car when she saw Jordan coming down the front steps and hurrying toward her, a thunderous frown on his face.

He came to a stop beside her and stood there for a moment, watching her. Then he demanded, "What do you think you're doing?"

Tiana slammed the trunk lid closed and, gripping the key in her hand so tightly it almost cut into the skin, she faced him. "Isn't it obvious? I'm moving."

"Is it so terrible, living here?" he asked flatly.

Tiana turned to lean against the car, dropping her gaze from his rigid face. "You know it's become intolerable."

"Not for me," he said casually. "There have been moments when you found it not unpleasant too. You won't deny that, will you?"

She shook her head, her face still turned away from him. "But those moments have been few—and I don't want to have to live through more humiliation just for a few pleasant moments. I can't stay, Jordan. It won't work anymore."

"By humiliation, I suppose you are referring to what happened yesterday in the studio," he said quietly. "You're making too much of it, Tiana. This childish impulse to run away has Farrell wondering if he's done something to alienate you."

She darted an angry look at him. "I've already explained my reasons for moving to Farrell. He understands."

"Somehow I doubt that you have told him your real reasons," he said tightly. "You're acting impulsively. I'll help you take your things back into the house and you can take a few days to think this over."

She half laughed, half groaned. "You can't order me around, Jordan. I don't want to stay another few days."

His voice hardened. "I won't let you go."

She straightened and, whirling, walked around to the car

door. "There's no point in prolonging this argument. I'm going now. I'd appreciate it if you'd allow Farrell to come and visit me before he leaves for Stillwater."

Jordan stared at her, the high cheekbones almost forcing their way through his brown skin as he managed, with great effort, to keep his temper. Fury tightened the wide mouth. "I wish I'd finished what I started in the studio yesterday. Then you might have felt differently about leaving."

The harsh words were as painful as blows. Tiana wrenched open the car door, feeling the blood leave her face. Squaring her shoulders, she got into the driver's seat, slammed the door, and drove away, never looking back.

She would not have been surprised if Jordan had jumped into another car and followed her. She kept her eye on the rearview mirror all the way to the highway, but no car came into view behind her. She was traveling toward Tahlequah alone, carrying all her belongings with her.

Nancy's apartment, Tiana knew from previous visits, was in an eight-unit complex, a modern red brick structure about half a mile from the elementary school where both she and Tiana taught. The apartment consisted of four large rooms—living room, kitchen with dinette area, two bedrooms, and bath. Sliding glass doors led from the dinette end of the kitchen onto a small, walled garden-patio. Nancy had added blues and greens to off-white walls and soft forest green shag carpeting, creating an attractive, restful environment.

The redhead had apparently been watching for Tiana, for as soon as the car pulled into the parking area behind the apartment complex, Nancy scurried across the small lawn to meet her friend.

"Welcome, roommate!" she caroled gaily.

Tiana got out of her car, smiling, relieved to be away from the complicated tensions at Jordan's place, free, she told herself determinedly, to start a new life with Nancy's cheerful presence to buoy her up.

The two young women carried all of Tiana's things inside, across the living room and into the bedroom that would be Tiana's. The room had two large windows, at present screened only by venetian blinds, an attractive Danish modern bedroom suite, and the same green shag carpeting that covered the living room floor.

Nancy dropped a heavy cardboard box on the bare mattress and looked around the room, wrinkling her nose. "This room has been closed off, since I didn't need it and my decorating budget has been strained to the breaking point with what I've done to the other three rooms."

Tiana turned from hanging the last of her clothes in the ample closet and, going to the bed, lay down to test the mattress. "It will be fun decorating it to suit myself."

Nancy sat down beside the cardboard box and watched her friend push a stray wisp of dark hair away from her face. "When you called yesterday, you sounded upset about something. I thought . . ." Her voice died away as Tiana looked at her. "Gracious," she said, concerned, "you've got circles about your eyes. I've never seen you look so awful."

"I'm tired," Tiana forced herself to say, dropping the back of one hand to rest on her forehead. "I need a few days to get my act together."

"Jordan Ridge called here not five minutes before you arrived," said Nancy. "What if he calls again?"

"Tell him I'm out," said Tiana wearily. "Tell him I've moved to Turkey. I don't care what you say as long as I don't have to talk to him."

Nancy got to her feet. "You stay right there, kiddo. I'll fix us some ginger ale."

Tiana closed her eyes and lay unmoving until Nancy returned. "Here you are." She offered a tall, frosty glass and Tiana sat up, accepting the ginger ale and drinking thirstily.

"Maybe that'll make you feel better," said Nancy anxiously.

"I'm fine," Tiana said.

"Sure you are. Never mind that you look as though

177

you've been run through the wringer. Okay, so I'm a nosy redhead. Just tell me to mind my own business—not that I'll do it."

Tiana couldn't help smiling, her affection for her friend too strong to shut her out.

"I'm sorry, Nancy, but the last few days have been awful. Farrell has decided to move to Stillwater to go to college. Dale demanded that I either marry him immediately or—"

"Fish or cut bait, eh?" Nancy provided dryly.

"Yes, so I told him I couldn't marry him—and he didn't accept my decision with much grace." She took another long swallow of the cold ginger ale. "Well, suffice it to say that I just want to rest and get ready for the new term and forget this summer ever happened."

Nancy looked at her for a moment, then said quietly, "I have no doubt that you will get over missing your brother, and you certainly are well out of an involvement with our high-and-mighty vice-principal. But that's not what's really bothering you, is it?"

Tiana looked puzzled. "What?"

"All this talk about Farrell and Dale," Nancy said wryly. "That's only the unimportant stuff. You left out something. From the way you look, the way you sounded on the phone yesterday, something rather explosive happened out there in the country. Something involving Jordan Ridge, of course."

Tiana's mouth twisted with irony. "I told you that day at the restaurant that Jordan was the absolutely worst man in the world I could have fallen in love with, if I had any sense. Well, things have happened that only confirm that belief."

Nancy looked hard at her. "Do you mean he finally broke through your defenses?"

Tiana's face grew warm. "We didn't—well, do what you are thinking. But not because of any high principles on my part. Fortunately we were interrupted in time."

Nancy's expression was compassionate. "Tiana, I'm

sorry. I take it Jordan has done something that you can't forgive."

"Forgive?" Unhappiness and ironic humor turned her brown eyes to black. "He's abominable! He was still making demands, ordering me about right up until the minute I drove away from his house. You told me if he ever found out how I feel about him, I would need heaven's help. Well, you were so right!"

"What are you going to do now?"

"Do?" Tiana said despairingly. "What can I do? Refuse to take his calls. Lose myself in my work. Try to forget." She took a deep breath. "Thank goodness he's going to Paris in a couple of weeks. By the time he returns, his ego will have been restored, and he'll have forgotten all about me."

Nancy's green eyes regarded her with sympathetic warmth. "I suppose you're right. Well, now that you're here with me, I'll introduce you to some super men. We'll have dinner guests, a party."

"Not just yet." Tiana shrugged. "I need time to forget everything that's happened first."

Nancy nodded and turned the conversation to brightening up Tiana's bedroom.

12

Tiana spent the next two days unpacking, organizing dresser drawers, and glancing through Nancy's decorating magazines.

Jordan phoned several times, but she refused to take his calls. Finally, late in the evening of the second day, the doorbell rang. Since Tiana was cleaning up the kitchen after dinner, Nancy went to admit the caller.

Tiana, in the act of adding soap to the dishwasher, froze when she heard Jordan's voice.

"I want to see Tiana."

She couldn't hear what Nancy said, her voice was too low, but if Nancy was trying to send Jordan away, she didn't succeed. Tiana heard him demanding again to see her.

Nancy came to the kitchen door. "It's . . ."

"Jordan," Tiana finished, feeling panic brushing her like moth wings. "I heard."

"I think you'd better speak to him," Nancy told her. "I don't believe he will leave until you do."

All too familiar with Jordan's stubborn will, Tiana didn't believe he would either. She dried her hands and, running her fingers down her sides in an effort to smooth the wrinkles from her cotton shirt and shorts, she walked on unsteady legs into the living room.

"What do you want, Jordan?"

He looked tired. Lines of exhaustion slashed his cheeks on either side of his mouth, and his eyes looked irritated and cloudy. He was wearing summer cord trousers and a yellow knit shirt that looked rumpled enough to have been slept in.

"Why wouldn't you take my calls?" he demanded.

With considerable effort, Tiana met his furious gaze. "Because I didn't want to. I didn't want to talk to you, Jordan—and I don't now."

"Well, dammit, you're going to whether you want to or not!" The dark raging eyes flicked to Nancy, who stood near the kitchen door. "I'm sure you will excuse us, Miss Pearson."

Tiana glanced over her shoulder at her friend, whose green eyes met Tiana's questioningly. After a moment, Tiana spread her hands in a gesture of capitulation. "It's all right, Nancy. We won't be long."

Nancy threw Jordan a long, speculative look, then said to Tiana, "I'll be on the patio."

When she was gone, Tiana turned back to Jordan, who stood in the center of the room, his body held tautly, as if a spring were coiled inside him.

"It's the height of rudeness to force Nancy out of her own apartment," Tiana said tensely. "Say what you came to say and have done with it."

Wordlessly, he stared at her, and then he began to walk aimlessly about the room, his glance raking over furniture and draperies and stopping for a second on the framed modernistic prints on one wall. Tiana watched him, wondering what he was thinking and, in spite of her immense anger at his forcing his way into the apartment, concerned over the weariness she saw in his every line. The silence grew and seemed to throb between them with a life of its own.

"You—must be working very hard," she said haltingly.

He turned from his perusal of the prints and fixed her with a look that shook her. "No, I'm not working at all."

She had no way of knowing what he meant by that. Had he finished the paintings he would be exhibiting in Paris? Or did he mean something more by the flat, almost accusing statement?

182

As the silence drew out again, she sensed that he was having difficulty finding the words to say what he had come to say. Finally, he asked, "Are you still seeing Gregory?"

"I don't intend to discuss Dale with you," she retorted.

His hands clenched at his sides, and she felt again a faint whisper of fear. His lips thinned and then moved scornfully. "I'm not leaving until you answer my question."

"No!" she flung at him. "I'm not seeing Dale."

"Then you don't intend to marry him?" he persisted in the same dogged way.

She made a bitter sound. "That hardly seems likely, since I am no longer seeing him, does it?"

There was a barely perceptible relaxing of all his muscles. His dark gaze swept over her, finally coming to rest on her face in a lingering examination. "I should have taken you when I had the chance!" The words exploded in the room as if they had been forced from him.

"You told me that when I left your house," Tiana returned haughtily. "You didn't need to come here to say it again. I know what you want from me, Jordan. I have always known."

He took a step toward her and she backed away, putting a chair between them. "You don't know as much as you think you do," he said coldly. "If I'd taken you then, you would have agreed to marry me. You'd have felt duty bound to do so."

"Well, maybe you don't know as much as you think you do either. Modern women aren't as dedicated to giving their bodies only to their husbands as women used to be!" She hardly knew what she was saying. The only thing that was clear to her was that she wanted to hurt him, to make him feel as wretched as she did.

"I'm not talking about modern women, Tiana," he said levelly. "I'm talking about you."

"And you believe you know how I think—what I feel?" she inquired bitterly. "You presume too much, Jordan!"

With the agility of a panther, he circled the chair behind

183

which she was standing and grabbed her arms before she could move. His fingers dug into her skin and he gave her a shake. "Answer me, Tiana! Did you go to bed with him?"

"No!" Her eyes blazed into his. "Now take your hands off me!"

He let her go as abruptly as he had grabbed her, his arms falling to his sides, and stood looking down at her with a mixture of relief and pain in his face. *I hate him!* she thought with anguish. *He doesn't love me, but he doesn't want another man to do so either.*

"God, Tiana, I didn't mean to hurt you." He ran a hand jerkily through his black hair. "I didn't come here for that. I came to ask you again to marry me."

Free of his cruel grip, Tiana took a step backward, putting distance between them. It was torture being so close to him, close enough to see every tense line in his face, the quivering of a small muscle near the corner of his mouth, close enough to smell his lime-scented aftershave. Conflicting emotions tumbled inside her—hate and love somehow intertwined.

He was watching her intently, seeing she could not guess what in her face. "Will you marry me, Tiana?"

She hugged herself, running her hands along arms that felt suddenly cold with a chill that came from inside her. Not trusting herself to speak, she shook her head.

"I give you my word I'll never have other women."

She stared at him, longing to reach out and smooth the jerking muscle alongside his mouth, half-wishing that she could do what he asked, that she could settle for what he had to give.

She swallowed convulsively. "No," she whispered.

"After a year or two, if it doesn't work out, I'll give you a divorce. Say you'll marry me, Tiana."

She couldn't bear to see the pleading in his face another minute. She turned away, burying her face in her hands. "What a fool you are, Jordan! Why must you insist on humiliating me—both of us like this? No, no, no! I won't marry you!" Tears sprang to her eyes, and she kept her face averted, not wanting him to guess how deeply she was affected by his words.

She heard his sharp intake of breath, but he did not speak. Finally, she lifted her tortured face and screamed at him, "Go away, Jordan! Go away and leave me alone!"

He stared at her for long seconds, and then, moving stiffly, he strode from the apartment. Shaking uncontrollably, Tiana sank into a chair. She stared ahead, unseeing, until Nancy came into the room and put a comforting arm around her. Nancy's sympathetic understanding was too much for Tiana; she broke down and sobbed bitterly.

Several more days passed before Millie Carver decided to break her uneasy peace. She had allowed Farrell to sleep late that morning, determined to try to talk some sense into her employer. Jordan came to the breakfast table looking like walking death. His face was haggard, the eyes appeared sunken, and the irises that had always been so deep and intense had taken on a dullness that tore at Millie's maternal heart.

She set a plate of bacon and scrambled eggs before him. Then, hands on hips, she blurted, "I swore I wouldn't say anything, Jordan."

He snorted. "That's a switch."

"You needn't think you can shut me up with sarcasm, either." She watched him pick up a fork and toy halfheartedly with the eggs. "It's time somebody did something. You're going to be sick if you keep on this way."

He took a bite of egg and chewed disconsolately. "What are you talking about, Millie?"

"You're not working," she plowed on. "Oh, don't try to deny it. I know you still go to the studio every day, but you sit and stare out the window. I've seen you. From the looks of you, you're not sleeping either. You don't talk, except when Farrell or I badger you into it, and then, more often than not, you bite our heads off."

"Have a heart, Millie. Leave me be."

She cut him off. "I mean to have my say! What do you intend to do with the rest of your life, Jordan? Den up out here in the country alone like an old boar coon?"

His mouth twitched with amusement at her choice of similes. "You, of course, think this old boar needs a lady coon to make his life complete."

"I've thought that for a long time."

He shrugged and laid down his fork. He leaned back in his chair and heaved a sigh. "I know you have my best interests at heart, Millie. Thank you for that. But has it ever occurred to you that my problem might be something entirely different? Maybe I'm going crazy." This last was laced with light mockery.

The housekeeper bristled with impatience. "You're crazy, all right. Crazy in love. Why don't you admit it and stop being such a pigheaded Indian?" She shook her head, her eyes taking in his tense features. "I declare, Cherokees are the stubbornest Indians alive!"

"While Choctaws, on the other hand, are the soul of patient reason," he drawled.

She ignored the jibe, intent on her own purposes. "You and Tiana both are so stubborn, you'd stand in the street and let a car run you down before you'd move if you took it into your thick heads not to."

"So," he returned, still drawling, "Tiana is the female with whom you, in your superior wisdom, have decided I'm crazy in love?"

"It's as plain as the nose on your face," Millie declared.

"I'm curious to know how you came by this gem of knowledge. You're not going to drag out that tiresome old saw about woman's intuition."

"Woman's intuition's got nothing to do with it," retorted Millie. "No, I got it straight from the horse's mouth—*you.*"

He laughed shortly. "First I'm a coon, and now a horse! But, you're not making any sense, old girl. I never told you anything of the kind."

"Yes, you did." Millie practically chortled. "Not with

186

words—with your paintbrush. It's all there in that portrait, Jordan—the way you feel about Tiana—for all the world to see. No man could have brought that portrait to life the way you did, made that girl so lovely and dewy-eyed, unless he was in love with her."

Jordan's gaze was absorbed. "I'm impressed, Millie. I didn't know you were a connoisseur of art."

"I don't know much about art, but I know love when I see it," she informed him smartly. "Now, why don't you come to your senses and go talk to Tiana. It won't hurt you to humble yourself a little."

The sound he made was brittle. "Millie, you would be amazed to know how much I have humbled myself already."

Indeed, this did seem to disconcert the housekeeper. "You don't say so."

"But I do," he replied, an ironic twist to his lips. "I swore never to look at another woman. I even said she could have a divorce if things didn't work out."

Millie's mouth fell open. "That's it? That's what you told that poor girl?"

"Yes, and it was the hardest thing I ever did, believe me. But she still turned me down."

"Lord, Jordan!" She reached for the coffeepot absently and refilled his cup. "For a man who's supposed to be such a hit with the ladies, you're about as romantic as a fence post! A woman doesn't want to hear such as that when she's being proposed to. She wants to hear that the man *loves* her." Millie's look was suddenly pitying. "Is that so hard to say?"

Surprisingly, he looked embarrassed. "It is when you've never believed in love."

"Pshaw!" Millie suddenly busied herself at the sink. "You go take another long, hard look at that portrait, and then tell me you don't believe in love." She glanced over her shoulder, where Jordan had sunk into morose silence. "And if you don't start eating something, I'll be burying you instead of trying to marry you off."

* * *

The weekend before Farrell was to leave for college, Jordan allowed him to stay with Tiana at the apartment, where he slept on the living room couch. It was a special two days for Tiana, during which she served Farrell his favorite dishes and shared his enjoyment over being rid of his cast. In celebration, they swam and went roller skating, laughing together, for the first time more as equals than as big sister and kid brother. Tiana's heart swelled with pride at the signs of maturity she saw in her brother, and it throbbed with pain, too, when she remembered that they would soon be separated and that, by the time she saw him again, he would be well on the way to being his own man.

But the pain was acceptable because Farrell was becoming the person she had always known he could be, and she had Jordan to thank for that. But she did not want to think about Jordan, and she succeeded surprisingly well in keeping him out of her thoughts most of the time.

The weekend passed quickly, and on Monday Farrell made the trip to Stillwater. Jordan had promised to drive him, he had told Tiana. During the remaining few days before the start of the term, Tiana kept very busy planning attractive bulletin boards for her classroom and outlining the work she hoped to cover in the first days of school. Thus occupied, she could forget, for hours at a time, the empty unhappiness of her personal life.

On Saturday night, before the start of school on Monday, Nancy went out with one of her frequent dates. Having the apartment to herself, Tiana showered and shampooed her hair, then did some hand laundry, filling with pantyhose and filmy underwear the wooden folding rack Nancy kept in the bathroom.

Dressed for bed in a nightgown and terry robe, Tiana settled down to watch a television movie. It was one she had wanted to see but missed in the movie houses, and she had been looking forward to viewing it in her own living room.

Barely ten minutes into the story, however, the doorbell

rang. Frowning her displeasure, Tiana considered ignoring the bell; it was probably one of Nancy's boyfriends. But the caller persisted, ringing the bell again and again until, sighing, Tiana hurried to the door and called, "Who is it?"

"Jordan."

All thought of the anticipated movie and everything else fled from her mind, and her heart thudded its dread in her ears. "I can't let you in, Jordan," she managed finally. "I'm ready for bed."

She heard his low curse, and then he said, "Do we have to go through this every time I call on you? Open the door before I break it down!"

With fingers that had suddenly gone cold, she raked long, silky strands of hair away from her face. Oh, God, why couldn't he leave her alone? But she knew he would do exactly as he had threatened if she didn't let him in. She opened the door, stepped back as he strode briskly into the room, then closed the door and leaned back against it.

He turned to face her, thrusting his chin forward. "I've just come from talking to Ben."

She blinked at him. "Ben? The superintendent? What has that to do with me?"

"He has agreed," Jordan went on imperiously, "to give you a month's leave of absence since a qualified substitute is available. All you have to do is call him and say the word."

Tiana's amazement was such that she felt suddenly dizzy, and there was a ringing in her ears. "Do you mean to say that you—you have been discussing some insane plan involving me with the superintendent of schools without even consulting me! Not that it would have made any difference if you had!" Her heart missed a beat as she stared at him. "You're mad! Jordan, I warn you, if you have jeopardized my job . . . What did you say to him?"

Jordan watched her, then said distinctly, "I told him, if things went as I hoped, you would be with me in Paris for the next month on our honeymoon."

She continued to stare at him, half on the point of tears,

189

half hysterical with laughter. "You *are* mad," she said weakly.

"That's one explanation," he said, his jaw hard, "for the utter and complete idiot I am making of myself over you. I haven't been able to work since you left my house. I hardly sleep—and when I do, I dream of you." His eyes flickered over her, glimmering in the softly lighted room.

Jerkily, she whispered, "Jordan, please . . ." Her voice throbbed with a plea for compassion.

He took the few steps that brought him close to her, and pulled her toward him. "Don't fight me anymore, Tiana," he said in a thick tone.

She closed her eyes to escape the vision of his haggard, but dearly beloved, face. Her body was limp as his arms went around her.

"I mean to have you," he muttered roughly.

A tear trickled down beneath her closed lids, and she felt his body tense. "Don't cry, for God's sake," he said bitterly. "Do you find me so repulsive?"

Shaking, she wiped a hand across her wet cheeks. "You know that isn't true," she whispered and, sighing, she relaxed against him while his hand moved over her hair, stroking gently.

"You—you said that madness was one explanation," she said, his earlier words still troubling her. "We both know you're quite sane. But what other explanation is there for the fact that, no matter what I say, you won't leave me alone?" There was weary resignation in the words.

Jordan's hand stilled on her hair. He tilted her face so that he could see it clearly, his eyes probing. She looked back at him, the muted room lights softening her tear-stained face, but the brown eyes met his without wavering.

He breathed in sudden hoarseness. His hand held her chin still and she looked at him in submission. His dark eyes delved into hers until a long shudder passed through her body. Her skin, where he touched it, seemed to burn with heat. Jordan's arms tightened around her, pulling her closer against him and, with a groan, she met his kiss with a hungry response that elicited a slow, sweet exploration of her mouth by his.

He broke off the kiss, breathing hard, cradling her head in the hollow of his neck and burying his face in her hair. "Oh, Tiana," he said unsteadily, his breath warm in her hair, "I adore you. I love you. I'll always love you, darling."

For a moment, she did not move or speak. It felt almost as if her heart had stopped beating.

"Did you hear me, Tiana?" The husky words echoed in her ears, and inside her a sweet turmoil was churning. At last, a trembling cry of pleasure rose to her lips.

"Oh, Jordan . . . Jordan!" She lifted her head and looked lovingly into his face. His eyes, veiled by their dark lashes, burned into her. She ran a finger along his mouth, then kissed it adoringly.

"I thought you didn't believe in love."

"I didn't," he admitted humbly. "You made me believe in it. Whenever I thought of you with Gregory—or any other man—when you kept refusing to marry me, it hurt so much that I knew it had to be more than just desire. Every time I looked at you, I wanted to hit you or make love to you. I wished we were back in the primitive tribal days so that I could drag you to my tent and announce that you were my woman." His voice broke off, shaking. "Oh, God, I can't live without you any longer!"

She felt a pulse throbbing in her throat, and she kissed him again, putting all of her love into the soft yielding of her lips. "Jordan, darling, I love you . . ."

He held her tightly, hurting and comforting her at the same time. "And you will marry me—at the first possible moment?"

"Yes," she murmured happily, snuggling her head against his shoulder.

He sighed and stroked her cheek with a trembling hand. Then a laugh rumbled in his chest. "You should have held out a few minutes longer. As a last resort, I was prepared to bribe you."

She lifted her head and looked up at him, her head to one side, her lips curved in a gentle smile. "All I ever wanted was your love. Once you offered me that, I couldn't say no." She paused. "But just for the record, what were you prepared to offer me?"

A teasing twinkle glinted in his dark eyes. "The painting you said you wanted, 'The Old Ones.'"

She gasped. "The one with Grandfather in it!" Her voice quivered with delight. "Oh, Jordan, you will give it to me, won't you? As a wedding present?" She cupped his face in her hands and kissed him seductively.

He gave a long groan of pleasure. "Tiana . . . my love, my life . . . the painting is yours. And so am I."